I0741847

Books by Edison T. Crux

Tale of the Wisconsin Werewolf
Tale of the Gévaudan Beast
Tale of the Twin-City Vampires

Websites

edisontcrux.com   •   enoctales.com

wisconsinwerewolf.com   •   twincityvampires.com

Edison T. Crux

Tale of the
Gévaudan Beast

An Enoc Tales Novella

Enygma Enterprises
Rockford, IL

Enygma Enterprises
P.O. Box 1284 Beloit, WI 53512
www.enygma-enterprises.com

The Enygma Enterprises name and logo are trademarks of Enygma Enterprises.

Cover design by Edison T. Crux.

Publisher's Cataloging-in-Publication Data
Crux, Edison T.
Tale of the Gévaudan Beast / by Edison T. Crux.—1st ed. p. cm.
Summary: Facing the impending death of his beloved wife, renowned neurologist Dr. Connor Amon will stop at nothing to find a cure for her terminal condition..
ISBN 978-0-9858873-5-3
[1. Supernatural — Fiction.] I. Crux, Edison T.   II. Title.

This book is dedicated to everyone who battles a terminal illness.

You face your demons with more courage than I can imagine.

Contents

Prologue
Sanity
1

Chapter 1
Eleanor
2

Chapter 2
Creutzfeldt-Jakob Disease
12

Chapter 3
The Devil's Physician
24

The Book of the Beast

Part 1
31

Part 2
44

Chapter 4
Moyset
59

Chapter 5
The Halloween Hunt
67

Chapter 6
A Devil's Bargain
78

Chapter 7
Heart Stopper
85

Chapter 8
What Would Eleanor Do?
90

Chapter 9
The Horseman's New Mount
99

Epilogue
Love
105

Prologue:
Sanity

Let me start by saying this; I am not insane.

I cannot blame you for thinking that I am. I certainly would, if I heard the tale I'm about to tell. I have wandered outside the realm of the sane world. If I survive this night—and I doubt that I will—people will surely call me a madman.

What I saw was insane. But I am not.

By the end of this story, I'll let you decide what I am. You might think me a lunatic. Or a coward. A monster, even. Perhaps that would be closest to the truth, although you must understand the reason behind all this madness.

When I'm gone, people will talk. A million rumors and stories about the old doctor who fell from grace.

But please, judge me only by the facts. I will tell you the whole story, if you are willing to listen.

I am Dr. Connor Amon, and this is my tale.

Chapter 1:
Eleanor

Every great story starts with a girl.

In mine, her name was Eleanor.

I remember the first time I saw her. It was my sophomore year at Elkhorn Area High School. This was a long time ago, mind you; If I recalled correctly, the year was 1955. She moved to Wisconsin from the east coast. I heard *about* her before I met her. Rumors spread of a new girl with exceptional grades and ambition. The way people spoke, I expected her to be a shy academic, much like myself.

But Eleanor Livermore was beyond anyone's expectations.

True, at first glance you might mistake her for your typical bookworm. Thick glasses. Hair that was smooth but not styled. Plain clothes. And standing at 5' 3", you would think she would vanish into a crowd unnoticed.

Five minutes in a room with Eleanor would change your mind about that.

She had an aura of confidence that commanded

Chapter 1

attention and respect, regardless of appearance. Her grades were the result of intensity. She was not afraid to speak up in class, and ask provocative questions. Many times she seemed to know more on the subject than the teacher.

I grew to admire her. And in no time at all, admiration turned to affection.

You see, Eleanor was everything I *wanted* to be. My grades were good, sure. And I got along fine with my peers. But I lacked that confidence.

I wanted to understand her. To find the source of her drive.

But most of all, I just wanted to be near her.

When Eleanor started a debate club, I got my chance. I signed up immediately, although I was never the debating type.

I spent sophomore year in her club. And I must confess; I didn't win a single debate.

Truthfully, it was because I was distracted. Eleanor debated with such conviction. When I was around her, she was all I could think about.

Admiration became a full-fledged, head-over-heels crush.

At the last meeting before summer, she pulled me aside. My heart hammered at her touch.

"You signed up for next year," she said. Her intense eyes were locked on mine. "No offense, but you're a terrible debater. Why do you keep showing up?"

Oh, how I loved her directness! She said exactly what she felt.

I blurted out my answer. "I come to see you."

Eleanor stared at me, and my face turned scarlet. I didn't intend to be so honest. I was embarrassed beyond measure, so when she didn't say anything I left with my head down.

Eleanor

I would have the whole summer to wallow in shame.

Two weeks after school was out, there came a knock on my door.

I was not expecting company, but my dad and little brother were busy in the shop. So I answered the door, expecting a salesperson or a friend of my parents.

What I saw was Eleanor Livermore, her arms full of books.

Before I could believe what I was seeing, she said, "May I come in?"

I nodded, and she walked boldly into my home. As if this were perfectly normal, she took a seat on the couch.

"What are you doing here?" I asked. Realizing that sounded rude, I added, "It's, uh, nice to see you."

Eleanor didn't look up. She was busy hunting through her backpack and armload of books. Suddenly she started to chuck books at me. I barely managed to catch them.

"You're Eisenhower," she said, still either stacking books next to her or hurling them at me. "I'll be Stevenson. We're going to reenact the 1952 presidential campaign. I'll give you the winning candidate as a handicap."

I was flabbergasted! I couldn't understand why she would do this.

Then Eleanor stared at me. Her blue eyes twinkled like the ocean in the sun. They said more than her words. She let herself smile—just a little. It struck me how beautiful she was. Maybe others wouldn't use that word to describe her, but it was true. I was captivated by her.

Taking the seat opposite her, I said, "You're on, Stevenson."

We debated for hours. I had to constantly fact check with the books Eleanor brought. She, however, had most of

Chapter 1

her facts memorized. My parents were delighted that I had a study partner. Eleanor stayed for dinner, and my parents joined us for our final debate.

Despite losing in real life, Adlai Stevenson won the presidency at the Amon house. When I saw her to the door, she said, "Tomorrow, we're doing medical malpractice."

All I could do was smile. I lost the election, but I sure felt like a winner.

Instead of spending the summer ashamed, I spent it with Eleanor.

We weren't dating, of course. I lacked the courage to suggest it. But from these debates a wonderful friendship was born. We talked for hours after we closed the books. At first we kept to light conversations—about school, mutual friends, and small town news—but soon we found ourselves discussing serious topics.

She told me how her parents struggled with money. Despite that, they would do anything to help their daughter succeed. Eleanor was taught to set her goals high, and avoid the mistakes of her parents.

I told her about my family. In comparison, the Amons had it easy. My father founded B.R. Amon & Sons, Inc., a construction business that he hoped to pass on to his children. Our house was small, but our plates were always full.

Money wasn't our problem; it was ambition.

We would always be where we were, doing what we did. My father already spent twenty years in construction, and was content to continue. My brother, Barbason Jr., was barely in his teens and already joining the business.

Eleanor saw it, too. "You have to set a goal for your life," she explained one day. The summer was nearly over, and our minds were on school.

"A life goal?" I said. Such an idea never occurred to me. "What should this life goal be?"

"Doesn't matter," Eleanor explained. "You could be a lawyer. Or a doctor. You could even be a college professor like I'll be. But you need to choose *something*. If you don't, the choice will be made for you, and you will be working at B.R. Amon your whole life."

I shuddered at the thought.

"Being a doctor might be fun," I mused.

Eleanor laughed. "You don't know the first thing about being a doctor, Connor."

"Fine, Miss Know-It-All," I said. "It was just an idea."

She looked me in the eye, suddenly serious. "Look into it. Spend this year deciding what you want with your life. But you need to make a decision by the end of the school year."

I saluted her. "Yes, ma'am."

Eleanor playfully punched my arm. "Watch your language, mister. It's 'Professor' to you!"

She gave me a hug. It was a gesture of friendship, of course. But all the same, my heart jittered.

"You can do anything," she whispered into my ear. "Anything you set your mind to."

The intimacy of her words struck a chord inside me. I was empowered. Knowing she believed in me, I felt that there was nothing I couldn't do.

Junior year was my best yet.

My grades jumped from *good* to *spectacular*. I took more classes. Joined more clubs. And the more I did, the better I got. The regulars at debate club were shocked by my

Chapter 1

impressive rhetoric. Even in social circles, this year people found me outgoing and charming.

And it was all thanks to Eleanor.

At every turn, she was there. She inspired me to work harder. To push myself to greater heights. To be the best I could. And by motivating me, Eleanor improved her own drive. Together, it seemed there was nothing we couldn't do.

We were an unstoppable team.

But Eleanor was a grade above me. This was her last year at Elkhorn Area High School. The thought terrified me. If she moved to go to college, our precious friendship might come to an end.

I was there when she was accepted into Harvard. Oh, what a mixture of emotions! On one hand, I was so happy for her; this was another goal accomplished. But if she went to Harvard, what would happen to our friendship?

As we celebrated her acceptance, it was my turn to look her in the eye. I said to her, "I'm going to be a doctor."

Eleanor smiled. "Finally decided?"

I nodded. "There's one more thing I decided."

"What's that?"

I forced myself to stay calm, although I confess my heart was pounding. "I want to be your boyfriend, Eleanor."

She began to laugh, and my spirits were crushed.

"Sorry," I pouted. "I didn't realize the idea was so silly."

The laughter slowed down. Eleanor stared at me with her ocean-blue eyes. "That's not why I'm laughing."

She took my hand.

"I laughed because I made a decision, too," she said. "I told myself that if you took charge of your life, and chased a real goal... Then I wanted to be your girlfriend. I wanted to very, very much."

A goofy grin crossed my face. I couldn't believe it.

Eleanor

Eleanor's smile grew warmer by the minute. "I guess we had the same goal, after all."

We kissed for the very first time. In that moment, I made another decision; I would love this girl for the rest of my life.

After that, everything was a blur.

Eleanor went to Harvard. I stayed in Elkhorn. The time apart was hard. The time together was wondrous. We celebrated my own Harvard acceptance. We tackled college with the same enthusiasm as high school. We were a force to be reckoned with, and among the best in every class we took.

On the day of my graduation, we made another decision. So in the summer of 1961, Eleanor and I became husband and wife.

Marriage did nothing to slow us down. Ours was a life of passion; and it seemed that the harder we worked, the deeper our affection grew. We were two people on a mission, and the energy of it all was intoxicating. We spent our days at grad school. Afternoons studying. And evening's in each other's loving embrace.

It was perfect.

The years flew by. She received her doctorate in Philosophy. I continued towards my chosen specialty; neurology. But something happened before Eleanor found a teaching position. Something we hadn't planned for.

Cassandra Amon, our beautiful baby girl, came into the world.

That's when Eleanor did something shocking. She decided to put her career on hold to stay at home with our daughter.

"But why?" I asked. "We could hire a nanny. Adjust our schedules. If anyone can make this work, it's us. You can

Chapter 1

still follow your dream."

She smiled at me, our precious child in her arms. "This *is* my dream," she said. "You and Cassandra. I'll have my chance for a career someday, when she's older. But if I go to work now... I will never get the chance to watch her grow."

My wife never ceased to amaze me.

"There is one condition, however," Eleanor said. Her eyes were suddenly sharp.

I was puzzled. "What is it?"

"You have to be the best," she said proudly. "Don't settle for being any old doctor. My husband will be the *top* neurologist. The best of the best."

That was that. When Eleanor made a decision, there could be no argument. "I can do that."

She kissed me, gently stroking my face. "I know you can."

And that's exactly what I did.

After years of rented apartments, we finally moved back to Elkhorn.

Not much changed here. My father still worked construction, now with the help of my younger brother. Poor Barbason. He was always a good kid, but so quiet and passive. I wondered if I would be working at B.R. Amon too, if it wasn't for Eleanor.

All the same, it was good to be home.

We spent our savings on a down payment for a house. It was small, but it was ours.

So much happened during these years. Thrills of parenthood. Challenges of med school. Struggles with money. I could spend hours reliving these joyous times.

However, I might only have hours to live. So I will hurry.

Eleanor

Cassandra grew into a beautiful young woman. She went to Beloit College, where she met John Lewis. Years later he proposed, and I got to walk my daughter down the aisle on her wedding day.

With Cassandra all grown up, Eleanor finally achieved her dream. She became a philosophy professor at Marquette University.

And I became a neurologist.

But I didn't stop there. I made a promise to be the best, and I wouldn't let my wife down. I wrote magazine articles. Funded research. Filled books with my personal studies. Through Eleanor's contacts at Marquette, I even struck a deal to revise medical textbooks.

The name of Dr. Connor Amon became synonymous with neurology.

But success takes time. Before I knew it, I was celebrating my 40th anniversary with my daughter and six year-old grandson. I couldn't believe it—me, a grandpa! I became an old man without realizing it.

Will was a wonderful little boy. He was so bright, just like his mother. And he was also shy, like my younger self. I wondered if someday, he would find his Eleanor; a woman who inspired him to be more than he thought he could be.

A grandfather could hope.

"Grandpa Connor," Will said, tugging at my sleeve.

Ever since he could talk, Will asked questions. By now I was used to his constant inquiries, and handled them with a smile. "Yes, Will?"

"How come you and Grandma Eleanor have been together so long?"

"That is a great question, Will," I said, ruffling the boy's hair. "We've been together because I love your grandma very, very much."

"What's loving someone very very much?" Will asked.

Chapter 1

This kid was something else! I couldn't stop myself from smiling. He had a better understanding of life at age six than many did at sixty. I knelt down, so that my grandson and I were at eye level.

"Will," I told him. "When you love someone that much, they become your whole world. Everything you do—*everything*—you do for them. You would do anything to see that special someone happy."

The boy looked in awe. Through his six year-old eyes, the task of loving someone that much was a heroic feat.

"One day, you'll find love like that," I declared.

"No way!" Will laughed.

I lifted him into my arms. He might say that now, but I knew better. There was a special lady out there for him. Someday they would find each other.

Maybe when that day comes, he'll understand just how far I went in the name of love.

The years were good to us. We had money. A family. Happiness. And a love that started in high school, and never stopped.

But three little words were about to tear everything apart.

Creutzfeldt-Jakob Disease.

Chapter 2: Creutzfeldt-Jakob Disease

I was a neurologist. Of course I saw the signs.

It started small. Eleanor forgot trivial things, such as the day of the week or a recent purchase.

Then came lack of coordination. Twice in one week, she lost her footing and fell.

When the jumpiness started, I truly got worried. She was sitting in her favorite chair. I came up behind her, to rub her shoulders as I have thousands of times. But this time, she screamed at my touch.

She was terrified.

It took half an hour to calm her. When she finally settled, she couldn't explain why she was alarmed.

"I... Wasn't expecting it," was all she said.

Then it happened again. We were sound asleep, but when I rolled over she let loose a gut-wrenching shriek. She fell out of bed before I was conscious.

Something was wrong.

I took her to Dr. Raksha, an old friend and colleague.

Chapter 2

Eleanor insisted that she was fine, but her eyes told a different tale; inside, she was still screaming. I braced myself for some form of dementia, perhaps the early stages of Alzheimer's.

If only we were so lucky.

Dr. Raksha uttered a three-word death sentence; Creutzfeldt-Jakob Disease.

My heart stopped. This was it, the worst-case scenario. CJD was incurable. Progresses quickly. Ravages your mind.

And is inescapably fatal.

There was less than a one in a million chance of getting CJD, and we were the unlucky winners. Dr. Raksha said she had less than a year to live.

One short, torturous year.

We didn't speak on the way home. What could we say? How do you respond to finding out you are as good as dead?

After Eleanor went to bed I lit a fire in the hearth. The big house already felt empty. I was left alone, to wander the halls of a house built on her enthusiasm. I tried to outrun my thoughts, but that's one race nobody wins.

When I could walk no longer, I broke down in tears.

Eleanor was my everything. She was my strength. My love. My motivation. Without Eleanor... I was nothing.

I never went to bed that night. I was too scared that I would frighten my wife with a touch. So I retired to the chair next to her, and watched her restless sleep. As I sat there, I made a decision.

I was Dr. Connor Amon, renowned neurologist. Her dedication made me the best in my field. Now, that skill was going to save her life. I *would* find a cure for CJD, before it

Creutzfeldt-Jakob Disease

was too late.

I just didn't know how.

Eleanor and I spoke with dozens of professionals, and visited countless research centers across the country. At every turn, we hit a dead end.

You see, Creutzfeldt-Jakob Disease is a complicated issue. Although many consider CJD to be the human form of "mad cow disease," that's not technically true. A variant form can arise from eating contaminated meat, but in Eleanor's case the disease was quite sporadic. It's caused by a buildup of abnormal prions in the brain, which quickly kill the brain's nerve cells. Under a microscope, I could see a pattern of tiny holes in my wife's brain tissue.

Once enough nerve cells die, so does the patient.

Eleanor was given Clonazepam to reduce muscle jerks and ease her suffering, but there was little else anyone could offer.

Despite our best efforts, Eleanor was slipping. She was less herself everyday. My strong wife was falling apart, and I was getting desperate.

Comfort came from an unexpected source; Barbason. My brother started to visit more after Eleanor's diagnosis. We were so different, it was hard to believe we were related. But aside from Eleanor, no one knew me better. He was right to worry about me.

"How ye holdin' up, Connor?" Barbason asked. He spoke with a rough country accent like our father. It was a style of speech I had long abandoned.

I wanted to tell him I was alright, but couldn't. You can only tell the same lie for so long before it wears on you.

"I'm lost," I confessed. "My whole life has been for her. Now… I just feel so alone. I don't know what I would

Chapter 2

do without her."

Barbason patted me on the back. Comfort was not his strong suit, but at least he tried. "I'll tell ye what ye'll do. Ye'll get by. It ain't gonna be fun and it ain't gonna be easy. But that's what Eleanor would want. She wouldn't want this to destroy ye."

He was right, of course. Eleanor would tell me to pick myself up, and carry on without her. And that was the problem; she was the strong one. Not me.

I couldn't live without her.

My search for a cure came up empty, but I wouldn't give up. I knew I would walk through Hell and back for Eleanor.

I just never thought it would come to that.

By chance I came across a name—Dr. Jacques DuPuis.

Apparently he ran a small clinic in a little French commune. There was no website or listing, but that happened with many small practices, especially overseas.

But the one mention I found was remarkable.

It was in a back issue of a French medical magazine. A man by the name of Delacroix saw him with a severe case of cancer. The next time he saw his primary doctor, Delacroix was inexplicably cured. The article said this wasn't Dr. DuPuis' first miracle, either; a decade earlier, he allegedly treated an Alzheimer's patient with complete success.

It sounded too good to be true.

But that was the extentof it. There was no word from the doctor nor his patients. This was particularly strange to me; in the medical field, this would have been a breakthrough. Cancer and Alzheimer's—two of the greatest challenges to modern medicine. Surely any treatment, experimental or otherwise, would have been published in greater detail. But no matter where I searched, nothing could be found.

Another dead-end, I thought, and put the idea of a miracle doctor out of my mind.

But it wouldn't last.

The next morning started as they all did now. I broke Eleanor's bacon and toast into bite-size pieces so she could eat them easier. Cereal was out of the question; her uncoordinated hands spilled more than she ate.

But as I prepared her food, she stared at me with a strange expression.

"Have some bacon, darling," I said.

She blinked. "Who are you?"

Those three words tore my heart in two. At that moment, it was as if I already lost her.

"I... I'm your husband," I answered.

"Oh."

That was it. She ate her breakfast as if nothing happened. I did my best to keep from crying. But in my sorrow, a crazy conviction came over me.

I would find Dr. Jacques DuPuis. And he would save my wife.

"And what do ye expect to find in France?" Barbason asked.

My brother was unpacking his suitcase while I packed mine. I asked if he would stay with Eleanor while I was away.

I closed my eyes. "The impossible; a cure. There's a doctor there who could help."

Barbason was skeptical. "It's been what—four

Chapter 2

months since she was diagnosed?" He put a hand on my shoulder. "Look, I know it's hard to accept, but don't ye think ye would be better off here, with her?"

"Here to watch her die?" I said.

"She *is* dyin', Connor," Barbason said, as gently as he could. "Instead o' spendin' the last months of her life flyin' around the world, maybe it'd be better if ye spend it with her."

I shook my head. "I'm going to save her."

"Connor," Barbason looked me right in the eye. "When are ye gonna accept the truth?"

In my heart, I knew he was right. But I couldn't face it. I snapped my briefcase shut. "Never."

He sighed, but didn't continue.

"Barbason," I said, putting my hands on his shoulders. "Take care of my girl while I'm gone."

His eyes were hard, but he nodded. He knew I was running. My little brother—with nothing more than a high school diploma—understood better than I did.

Before I knew it, I was at the Aéroport de Lyon-Saint Éxupéry outside of Lyon. The flight was only the first leg of my journey; I had many long miles of travel by train and road ahead. Traveling in a foreign country was humbling. I could read French fluently, but it had been decades since I spoke the language. I was out of practice, but I found myself getting better with use.

There is no beauty like the French countryside. I went through many lovely cities and towns, enjoying the culture. The further south I went, the fewertowns I saw. The road wound through vast mountains and fields. It was like traveling back in time, to a land less touched by civilization.

Finally, nestled amongst the mountains, was Mende.

Creutzfeldt-Jakob Disease

With only 12,000 residents, it was hardly larger than Elkhorn. But it was a metropolis compared to the miles of open country I had journeyed through to get here.

I spent the night at the *Hotel Du Pont Roupt,* a lovely little hotel on the river.

The next morning, my search began.

I had an address for this clinic, but couldn't find it on a map. My hope was that the locals could confirm its location. I first went to the receptionist, who was very cordial, even to this ignorant American. I asked (in the best French I could manage) if she knew of a Dr. Jacques DuPuis.

Suddenly, her expression changed.

"Je ne sais rien," she said. ("I know nothing.")

Her response was strange, but I didn't press the matter. I expected no trouble; surely someone would point me in the right direction.

As the day went on, I discoveredhow wrong I was.

I went to the visitor's center. The *Centre Hospitalier de Mende.* Even the local market. No matter where I went or who I asked, nobody would admit such a clinic existed. I would have believed them, too, if it wasn't for the look of fear in their eyes.

It was like they were hiding something.

I had dinner at the *Restaurant Grill de La Tour,* hoping some food and drink would ease my growing worries. After I ate, I joined the locals at the bar. Perhaps with a few drinks, the locals would loosen up.

"Est-ce que…" I said, pausing to think over my translation. *"Quelqu'un sait de docteur Jacques DuPuis?"*

The room went silent. All eyes fell on me.

"Le Diable médecin!" one man cried from down the bar.

"The… Devil's Physician?" I said in plain English. The man nodded vigorously, as if he understood.

Chatter erupted. I couldn't translate everything; they

Chapter 2

were talking too fast and their speech was too slurred. What little I could understand was troubling.

Evil!

The witch-doctor!

He is cursed, I say!

Practices Black Magick.

Devil's Physician.

Cursed!

"So…" I said, interrupting the commotion. *"Il existe?"* ("He exists?")

No one spoke. The brute of a man sitting next to me put a hand on my shoulder. *"Monsieur,"* he said slowly, making sure I understood. *"Pour votre propre sécurité, laisser ici. Le médecin que vous cherchez est un mythe."*

("For your own safety, leave here. The doctor you seek is a myth.")

Fearing a panic, I said no more. But I had confirmed one thing; Dr. Jacques DuPuis was real.

The next day I hired a taxi. I gave him the address and explained I wasn't sure of the exact location. The driver was wary. I sensed that he too might pretend he is ignorant, so I offered to pay double his rates, up front. Reluctantly, he took my money and we drove out of town. The road wrapped up the side of a mountain, with a great view of Mende.

To be honest, I wasn't entirely surprised by the locals' reaction. This land felt lost in time. Here, you could easily cling to the superstition of the past. Curing the fatally ill might be seen as witchcraft, and the doctor a devil worshiper. If he was a recluse by nature, that would only further this local belief.

But I had dealt with my share of unpleasant doctors.

Creutzfeldt-Jakob Disease

I wasn't afraid.

The road went on, rolling through woods and hills. It was a beautiful scene, but I must confess I was a little unsettled once the town was lost from view.

My driver was also getting nervous. He eventually pulled over and said, *"Gardez votre argent, américain. Je n'irai pas plus loin."*

("Keep your money, American. I will go no further.")

How unprofessional! I insisted this was silly, but the man couldn't be persuaded. He said if I followed this road, I'd find it. Thoroughly annoyed, I slammed the door shut and continued by foot.

Several miles I walked. It was rough going; the path went uphill, and my shoes were unfit for hiking. When I saw a building nestled among the mountain, I was overjoyed; that had to be it!

As I approached, I saw a sign on the door. If, after all this trouble, I ran into a "Sorry, we're closed" sign, I would have been devastated. But I regained my spirits as I translated.

Welcome!
Please excuse our lack of staff. If you would kindly register at the front desk and take a seat, the doctor will be with you shortly.
Thank you for your cooperation.

Interesting. I went inside, and found the place to be surprisingly modern. I expected some run-down facility, but this clinic was as clean as any in the States. The lobby was decorated with potted plants, white tile floor, and large

Chapter 2

paintings of France's finer cities. At the front desk a computer stood facing the lobby, with a message similar to the door.

All I had to do was enter my name, and I was in queue to see the doctor.

How wonderfully efficient! If Dr. DuPuis didn't have many patients (and I couldn't imagine he did), this automated system would keep his costs down by removing the need for staff. I took a seat, feeling better already.

To pass the time, I checked the reading material left out. There weren't any magazines, but the table was littered with newspapers and a bible. I picked up a paper and had a read.

It seemed there was a terrible accident at the 24 Hours of Le Mans motor race. One of the cars crashed, sending pieces of debris into the crowd. 8 spectators and the driver were killed, while 120 were severely injured.

But something was strange… This paper was dated June 13th, 1955. Why would he have such a dreadful back issue lying around?

I looked for something better to read, but noticed a trend. Another newspaper was dated September 22nd, 2001, with a front page article about a deadly chemical factory explosion. The one American publication was for December 16th, 1967, the day after the Silver Bridge collapsed in Point Pleasant, West Virginia. That accident led to forty six deaths.

I put the papers away. I lost my interest in reading.

There was something unsettling about those articles. If I didn't know better, I would have thought they were deliberately chosen to show great disasters. I took a better look around, hoping to ease my nerves.

The plant next to me wasn't doing so good. Many of the leaves were brown and eaten. When I touched the leaves, I made a strange discovery; the plant was plastic. And tucked

Creutzfeldt-Jakob Disease

away within the leaves was a hungry, plastic locust.

Why put a fake dead plant in a clinic?

My heart began to pound. I turned to one of the paintings. Paris was painted in remarkable detail, with the bustling streets and lavish buildings. But something was wrong... The people in the street weren't walking—they were *running,* and behind them stood an executioner with an axe. Decapitated bodies lay at his feet.

Panic crept through me. Nothing was as it seemed here. I began to feel like this whole clinic—from the friendly message to the benign décor—was all an act. A cheap mask to hide some horrific truth.

I reached for the bible, hoping to find comfort in its verses. But when I flipped it open, I gasped.

Every page in the bible was blank.

Beep.

The sudden sound nearly sent me into shock. There was a new message on the computer. Cautiously I approached the screen and read.

The doctor is ready.
Please follow the door to your right

A door creaked open, all on its own. I was filled with irrational fear, and had to fight the urge to run. The words of the locals ran through my mind, as dread quickly overcame me.

If it wasn't for Eleanor, I never would have walked through that door.

The hallway wasn't straight; it veered off at a strange angle. It made you off-balance, like one of those tricks at a fun house. Only this wasn't fun, not at all. I stumbled to the

Chapter 2

door with Dr. Jacques DuPuis' name on it.

Before I could knock, the door swung open.

"Hello, Dr. Amon," a voice said from inside. It spoke perfect English, without a trace of an accent.

I looked up and froze. A nightmare sat in the chair before me, its lips curled into a sinister grin.

"I've been expecting you."

Chapter 3:
The Devil's Physician

"Ex—expecting me?"

My voice quivered. But this man... He was perfectly calm. He sat, elbows on the desk and fingertips touching. Dr. DuPuis was around my age, in his late sixties or early seventies. He had round, rimless glasses and broad shoulders. But it's his grin that still haunts me; it was the smile of a maniac.

"Of course," he said. "I have ears in town. I heard a rumor you were coming to see me."

I felt foolish. I asked dozens of people in Mende for directions here. He could easily have gotten wind of my arrival.

Attempting to steady my breath, I offered my hand. DuPuis' grip was firm.

"I apologize," I said. "My reaction was rude. I'm afraid you are not very popular in town, and the locals made me expect, well…"

"A monster?" he interrupted.

Chapter 3

"Yes… I suppose that's right." I was still nervous, and couldn't explain why.

Dr. DuPuis' laugh cut through the air. My heart rate shot up at the sound. "People around here have a history of superstition. Do not mind their rambling. Now then, doctor… What can I do for you?"

I gulped. Here, at the end of the road, I was afraid to say it. "I'm looking for treatment for Creutzfeldt-Jakob Disease."

"I see," Dr. DuPuis said, an eyebrow raised. "I take it you already know thediagnosis is bleak?"

"Yes, I am aware of that."

"I am not an easy man to find."

"I am aware of that, as well."

Dr. DuPuis smiled. "Venturing across the sea and through the mountains to get here. You American doctors are so devoted!"

The joke didn't strike me as funny. "I did it for my wife."

"She asked you to come?"

"No. She has CJD."

The room went silent. Dr. DuPuis stroked his chin. "I see," he said. "You love her, then?"

It was a strange question. No other doctor had asked. I wanted to appear professional, but I was caught off guard.

A tear fell down my cheek as I said, "Yes… I love her very much. She…" My voice crackled with emotion. "She's going to die if you can't help her."

Had I really traveled 4,300 miles to whimper in front of a stranger?

The doctor observed me closely. I felt painfully naked in front of him, as if he could see all the sorrow running through me. He didn't speak, just looked me up and down.

"Do you… Know of any treatment?" I asked.

The Devil's Physician

After a long pause, he finally said, "There is no medical cure for Creutzfeldt-Jakob Disease. Not in America, and not here."

My heart sunk. But this was my last hope, and I couldn't accept it was over. "Please! I've heard of your past successes. What about Delacroix? His cancer was untreatable, yet it all but vanished after coming to you. Or, what about the Alzheimer's sufferer who you allegedly cured? Did you turn them away so easily?"

DuPuis chuckled. "You've done your homework, doctor. But I'm afraid you can't always trust the tabloids. I didn't cure Delacroix of his cancer, nor Mr. Plourde of Alzheimer's."

I was devastated. "B—but… I thought they recovered."

"Oh, they did."

Now it was *my* turn to raise a brow. "How?"

"The power of prayer," he said. A twitch of a grin crossed his lips.

Great, I thought to myself. *He's religious.*

"You don't think I've tried that?" I slammed my hands on his desk. "Every night since I found out. *Every—single—night!* I prayed to God for an answer. For *anything* that could save her!"

Despite my anger, DuPuis was stoic as ever. "Therein lies the problem."

I glared at him. "What does that mean?"

"It means *your* God won't help."

His words sent a chill down my spine. Suddenly, images flashed across my mind—of the newspapers. The dead plant. The morbid painting. The empty bible.

DuPuis stood up. He strolled around his desk, letting one hand caress the wood as it passed. "Doctor, don't ask the Creator for miracles. If He even exists, He has long stopped

Chapter 3

caring about sinful little humanity."

Wind rattled the windows. Was this more religious rambling? Maybe... But in this isolated land, the concept sounded all too possible.

"Then who do you pray to?" I asked. "Satan?"

That shrieking laugh again. "Now, now, doctor." He stood directly in front of me, and I noticed his imposing height. I had to look up to meet his eyes. "You came here seeking miracles, which I so happen to know a thing or two about. Why so quick to judge my methods?"

"I… I'm sorry." I stared at my feet. "It's just… I'm so afraid I'll lose her."

DuPuis put his hands on my shoulders. His skin was cold to the touch.

"You will lose her," he said softly. "This disease will destroy your wife in the worst way possible. It will strip her of everything she is. Then, when she is nothing but a husk of her former self, she will die. And you will have to watch."

All my worst fears, confirmed.

"You will watch because you love her too much to look away. You can't abandon her, but you can't save her either. So you will stand by her side, hoping it gives her some comfort. But in your heart, you know; she has already forgotten you. Your presence will comfort her no more than a stranger's, because that's all you are now—a stranger. But you won't leave. You'll torture yourself until she finally dies. Then… It will be your turn to be a husk."

Misery suffocated me. Tears poured down my face.

"This is what will happen if you do not take my advice. My alternative will not be easy, and the price will be heavy. But, really… What have you got left to lose?"

"Nothing…" I mumbled.

"Nothing," DuPuis repeated. His voice was almost a purr; gentle, soothing, and strangely eerie. "That's all you are without her. So, if it costs everything you are, then it really costs nothing at all. Isn't that right, Dr. Amon? The choice should be quite simple."

I didn't have the strength to respond. I was a wreck. In all my life, never had I felt so insignificant. After all—was he wrong?

"What do I have to do?" I said.

An insane smile crossed DuPuis' face. "I was waiting for you to ask."

I couldn't believe what I was doing.

Instead of finding experimental treatment, I found myself hiking further up the mountain. Dr. DuPuis lent me a pair of hiking boots, a flashlight, and other supplies. It was as if he *knew* he'd be sending me into the wilderness.

Or, maybe, I wasn't the first to be sent.

Already I was tired. The clinic was three miles downhill, and I could only guess how much longer I had to go. I feared I would collapse before I made it.

("This disease will destroy your wife in the worst way possible.")

The cruel words echoed in my mind. He was right; I had nothing left. If this journey destroyed me… At least I would die trying.

At last I reached the end of the road. It wasn't a dead end, not really; more of a sharp turn around and back up the mountain. I abandoned the road, and walked on.

When I reached the edge of the mountain, the view took my breath away.

There was nothing but vast, open countryside as far as the eye could see. It was the kind of scene you only saw in pictures—or dreams. It was absolutely beautiful, and untouched by the passing centuries.

Chapter 3

But could these mountains be home to the Devil?

This day made me superstitious. Can you blame me? Before I came here, I would have thought this talk ridiculous. But that was before I met Dr. DuPuis. Now, his laugh haunted me and filled me with doubt. I understood why the locals called him the Devil's Physician—he hardly denied it himself.

Devil or no devil, it didn't matter. I was willing to damn myself for Eleanor.

The sun started to set. I should have set up camp for the night, but adrenaline forced me onward. I trekked on, following the setting sun. By the timeI reached the forest, it was gone; I walked by the light of a bright moon.

Navigating the woods proved challenging. I was quick to lose my way, and before long couldn't tell east from west.

I was lost.

This was the wilderness, and I was no woodsman. Unlike the tame Wisconsin farmlands, real predators hunted these woods.

I began to panic.

Trees seemed to close in on me. Danger could be around any corner, and I wouldn't know until it was too late. I wanted to turn back and run... But I didn't even know which way *was* back. I wandered, fearing this would be the end of my story.

At last, I saw something.

("There is a cave, like a jagged scar across the cliff.")

Dr. DuPuis described it. I walked into a clearing, with the long-gone remains of a bonfire. A crooked rip opened up into the mountain.

("There, you will find what you seek.")

I approached the entrance, and heard an eerie whistling. Surely it was just the wind... But it sounded alive. It reminded me of the story of the cyclops. I imagined the sound was the snoring of a man-eating giant.

I braced myself, clicked on the flashlight, and went inside.

At a glance I knew this cavern had been inhabited long ago. Crude tables and benches lined the walls, and the floor was littered with bones of all sizes. They looked like animal bones...

At least, most of them did.

Some bones were disturbingly human. I tried not to think about the cave's grisly past. It might have been home to thieves. Or bandits.

Maybe even cannibals.

There were few artifacts left behind. Whoever was once here either took their belongings with them, or never had much to begin with.

One thing stood out, however. There was a book, sitting alone on a table.

I examined it. This book was ancient; its leather peeling and its pages yellow. There were no words on the front or back, but on the spine I found the title.

Livre de la Bête. The Book of the Beast.

I shivered. There was something ominous about it. It was just another corpse in this boneyard, yet I swear there was life in it. Holding the book gave me the sensation of handling a serpent; it felt cold, scaly, but unmistakably alive.

Could this be what Dr. DuPuis sent me to find?

There was only one way to find out. I took the book outside, and read under the light of the moon. The pages were brittle, and the handwritten French slow to translate.

But the story it told changed my life forever.

The Book of the Beast

Part 1

This is the Tale of the Gévaudan Beast.

As record keeper of the *Cercle de la Bête*, it is my task to preserve our history and rituals. These events I have either witnessed first-hand, or are the stories passed directly from those who were involved.

The 6th of May, 1764, the Dark Horseman came to us.

Françoise Traverse was visited by this deity in her sleep. He appeared to Françoise as an angel, but not one from Heaven; this was a Dark Angel, a soldier from the legions of Hell. He spoke to her with a serpent's voice.

"Fine lass, I ask thee for your hand in marriage."

Of course, Françoise was stunned! This apparition exuded power; one could not help but kneel in His presence. Yet she hesitated.

"And for what reason shall I take thee as a husband, mighty shade?" Françoise asked.

The angel looked at her with hellfire eyes. "*Power,*" He said. "*Revenge. And pleasures the likes of which you have never known. I know you, Françoise Traverse. I know of the seed which was lost, and the barren womb which shall never bear another.*"

He spoke true; for Françoise had miscarried many times, the most recent only days earlier. She was left with emptiness, and a longing for children she may never have. Her husband grew impatient as well, and she suspected he was unfaithful to her.

"You cannot quell the sorrow in me," she said.

"*Misery cannot be destroyed. But, with my help, it can transform.*"

At this, Françoise was intrigued. "Transform into what?"

"*Fury,*" said the apparition. "*You will become an avatar of anger, the embodiment of hatred. Your fury will be so great, it will block out the sorrow. All you will feel is rage, and the immeasurable satisfaction that comes from watching the world tremble before you.*"

Françoise considered his proposal, but not for long. Release from her sadness was too tempting of a bargain.

"Very well," said she. "I accept your proposal, mighty shade."

So that night, a dark ceremony took place. Françoise and the angel, whose name was Moyset, were wed. They were bound more tightly than any mortal couple could; for their union was of the soul.

True to His word, Françoise was transformed. Hatred eclipsed her sorrow, and she became something more than human.

She was the *loup-garou*—a werewolf.

No words could describe the change. Françoise now saw the world through a predator's eyes. Her Dark Husband was with her always, nestled in the core of her black heart.

Of all the blessings of Moyset, perhaps His greatest was known as The Gift. He would merge with Françoise, and become the legendary Beast—the Hellhound. This was not a transformation of the body, but of the soul; for the human form was shed, and the spiritual monster was freed. Françoise craved The Gift. It was only then that she could lose herself completely to rage.

There was one problem, however; her mortal husband. With her new senses, Françoise smelled the musk of other women on him.

"Please, Master," she pleaded with Moyset—her *true* husband. "let me leave him for good. I do not love him. Not as I adore you!"

From the darkest corner of her mind, she heard His slithering voice. *"No,"* said He.

Françoise sulked. "But why, my Lord?"

"Because," said Moyset. His voice was silky. *"One must never walk away... From a meal."*

So Françoise was given The Gift, and her hellish fury devoured the man she once loved.

She was liberated, and now she could take on her true purpose; to wipe the world clean. This was a world of suffering. It was mercy to end it, not just for herself but for everyone. An empty world cannot weep.

"What now, my Lord?" Françoise asked.

"Now," He answered. *"We find the others. Broken souls such as yourself, who see the world for what it is—worthless. We will find them, and forge our own covenant. Then, together... We will send this planet plunging into the abyss."*

Françoise roamed with the speed of an animal. She slept in the woods, unafraid—none of God's creatures dared strike her. She was on the hunt, following her nose for the feelings of man. In the air she tasted greed, lust, and anger, but it was sorrow she sought. For that, she could offer relief.

Françoise's hunt led her to the Mercoire forest, outside of Langogne. Misery called to her from miles away, and brought her to a small home by the forest. As her body lay outside, her spirit went through the walls to find the source.

A boy, still just a teenager, wept in his room. In one hand was a lock of hair; in the other, a painting of a young woman.

"Why? Oh, why have you done this, Marie?" the boy cried. "Why must you leave me?"

Françoise didn't need to hear the whole story; she could taste it on the boy's breath. Marie was his sweetheart, and she was no longer interested in him.

Perfect.

There came a tapping at the window. The boy jumped, and saw a figure peering in at him. Françoise was unlike anything he had seen; she had become wild and unkempt, the apparition of a savage goddess.

"What is thy name, child?" said Françoise.

The boy wiped his eyes. "Pierre," he said.

"Pierre, my dear child, I can feel your pain. But sadness is not the answer." Françoise had not spoken in days. Her words now carried the deep reverberation of a deity.

The window flew open in a gust of wind.

"Come." Françoise extended her hand. "Sorrow leads you nowhere. I will show you the path to freedom."

Reluctantly, Pierre took her hand. The moment they touched, the Devil climbed in through the boy's fingertips.

For the first time since their marriage, Françoise could not feel her Dark Husband within her. But she did not worry. As He slipped into the boy He whispered *"Fear not; for it is to you that I will always return."*

For Pierre, the moment was empowering.

Devilish tendrils crept through his veins. They were utterly alien, yet with them came a sense of power. When this feeling snaked its way up his spine, Pierre heard the dark angel's voice for the first time.

"Let go, childe. Shed this fleshy vessel, and let me grant you a body of vengeance."

Pierre abided, and he too was given The Gift. The Beast roared from the room and into the woods. He needn't think of where he was going. Just as the heart knows to beat, Pierre's legs knew where to take him. He was at Marie's cattle ranch within seconds, glaring at her from the tree line. She was as beautiful as ever, which only intensified his fury.

The boy in Beast's clothing charged from

the Mercoire forest. Livestock yipped and scattered. Marie screamed. But before Pierre reached her, the bulls stepped in. They fought him off with their horns, and Pierre was unfamiliar with his new form. In those seconds lost, Marie escaped. Pierre retreated into the forest, defeated.

"Do not fret, my son," said the voice in his veins. *"She is of no importance now. You can take out your anger on everyone we pass. To you, each victim will bear her face, and you can slaughter her a hundred times over."*

And so, Pierre returned to his body and Moyset returned to Françoise. They traveled, seeking others like them.

They were the *Cercle de la Bête*—the Circle of the Beast.

This is when I came into the story.

It was the middle of July, and I was a wreck. My legs had been trampled in a riding accident, and the doctors said I would never walk again. I would spend the rest of my miserable days bedridden.

My frustration called to them.

They found me at my home. Françoise was a vision of power. Like the boy, I saw her less as a person and more as a goddess. She called herself The Devil's Bride. Pierre had changed as well; there was a murderous glint in his eyes.

"My Husband can grant you legs," Françoise said.

It was impossible to refuse. I was a cripple, and saw the limits of mortality. We are all just one meaningless accident away from death. So when these creatures—for they were no longer human—offered a second chance, I couldn't turn away.

Françoise kissed my lips, and the Dark Horseman rode down my breath.

There is no greater blessing than to be host to Moyset. For He is mighty, and the world trembles at His feet. I abandoned my ruined body. For that day, I was the *Loup-Garou*. The Hellhound.

The Beast.

I killed a woman that night. I do not know her name, or what sort of life she had. In that moment, I was finally free. Virtuous or vindictive, it mattered not—I took what I pleased, and didn't feel a touch of guilt.

The Dark Horseman stayed with me for many days and many nights. Together, we rained terror and death from these woods. And my human body was slowly healing. Within weeks I could shamble with the aid of a cane. After a mere month, the only sign of my injury was a slight limp.

Once I was mobile, Moyset returned to His bride, and the Circle of the Beast moved on.

We plagued the French countryside with our attacks. *la Bête du Gévaudan*—the Beast of Gévaudan—was known throughout the land. We drowned our sorrow in blood, leaving a trail of slaughtered women and children in our wake. The boy, Pierre, was even allowed to claim his right of manhood on some victims.

Although Moyset was our true master, we worshiped Françoise with nearly the same reverence. She was our one link to her Dark Husband. Without her, that connection would be lost forever.

The Circle of the Beast grew in numbers. We performed rituals to please the Great Moyset. In this way, we all took part in The Gift—even though it was rarely given to anyone besides Françoise.

I have recorded our most important rituals below.

Rite of Summoning

My sons and daughters!
This powerful Rite shall call me forth from the netherworlds, and grant you audience with your Dark Master.
Here is what you need:
The Seal of the Great One, drawn inside a Circle of Invocation (shown below).

One basin of water, placed in the center of the Invocation Circle.
One *athame*, or ritual dagger.
Six wax candles, placed at each point of the Circle.
Then the Host must stand in the center of the Circle. All present must recite the following incantation:

<h1 style="text-align:center">Part 1</h1>

"Tis night! 'tis night! and the moon shines
white,
The shadows stray through burn and brae, and
dance in the sparkling rill.
'Tis night! 'tis night! and the Devil's light
Casts glimmering beams around
The maras dance, the nisses prance
On the flower-enamelled ground.
'Tis night! 'tis night! and the werewolf's might
Makes man and nature shiver.
To the great Moyset, I have this to say;
Thy presence please deliver!
A boon I ask thee, mighty shade,
Within this circle I have made.
Haste, haste, haste, lonely spirit haste!
Here, wan and drear, magic spell making,
Findest thou me—shaking, quaking.
I pray you send hither,
Send hither, send hither,
The great grey shape that makes
men shiver!
Shiver, shiver, shiver!
Come! Come! Come!"

At the end of the incantation, I shall present
myself to my followers.

The Book of the Beast

Rite of Becoming

Sons and daughters!
Once I stand before you, it is time to speak thy
request.
Perform this Rite after the Rite of Summoning
to ask me to grant you my most glorious Gift!
All present must chant:

Head of raven, hellfire eyes.
Atop His night-black horse He rides.
Tail of serpent, dead man's claw.
Teeth of razors to line your maw.
Oh Dark Horseman, born in the abyss,
Who taketh thy bride, by His frozen kiss.
Make me a werewolf strong and bold,
The terror alike of young and old.
Grant me a figure tall and spare;
The speed of the elk, the claws of the bear;
The poison of snakes, the wit of the fox;
The stealth of the wolf, the strength of the ox;
The jaws of the tiger, the teeth of the shark;
The eyes of a cat that sees in the dark.
Make me climb like a monkey, scent like a dog,
Swim like a fish, eat like a hog.
Softly fan me as I lie,
And thy mystic touch apply—
Touch apply, and I swear that when I die,
When I die, I will serve thee evermore,
Evermore, in gray wolf land, cold and raw.

At the end of these rituals, Françoise would abandon her human form, and take on the body of the Beast. Françoise would fall, unconscious, and her spirit rise from her body.

Then, her spirit would Change.

The Beast manifests before us, like an apparition. It is glorious to behold—our Master's power proven! She would let out a howl, then begin the hunt. Françoise took particular pleasure in the slaughter of women and children. For she could never be a mother, so she took out her fury on those she envied most.

It is said that Françoise would possess the body of a mundane wolf, to bolster her power. She could then fight with the physical form of the wolf, and the otherworldly might of the Beast.

It was an unstoppable force.

Part 2

In October of 1764, the Circle of the Beast was almost lost—and was reborn stronger.

While on the hunt, Françoise was attacked by two hunters. She fought them bravely, but their bullets shred the weak flesh of the wolf. She retreated to the woods, where the wolf soon died.

But the bond ran deep. We at the camp watched in horror as wounds burst upon Françoise' dormant body. When her spirit returned, she was terribly weak.

Françoise was dying. And so was our tie to the Dark Horseman.

What happened next, no words could do justice.

Without warning, our bonfire went out. A wintry breeze sliced through the air.

Light came from the extinguished ashes. Not firelight, no... This was moonlight. Pale white streaks of it spun round like a tornado. We were illuminated, but instead of heat these moonlight swirls froze the air around us.

At the center of the light, a silhouette stood.

We dropped to our knees. We could see nothing but the figure's eyes, but we knew who it was—Moyset, the Dark Horseman. None of us had seen Him, not like this. We heard His words through Françoise, but He had never granted us a true audience. We trembled in His presence.

"Fear not," said Moyset. *"for bullets of lead cannot vanquish the loup-garou. Naught but silver can, which must never be touched."*

So Françoise resumed the hunt. With each day, her mangled body repaired itself, until finally she was good as new.

Françoise had Risen. The Dark Horseman triumphed. And the Circle of the Beast continued its reign of terror.

We finally caused an uproar.

The king put a hefty ransom on the head of *la Bête.* Everyone was up at arms—peasants and nobles alike. They formed hunting parties, and scoured the land with spears and pitchforks and rifles.

An ordinary wolf would have fallen. Not us.

They didn't expect human intellect. We outsmarted them at every turn. Hundreds of wolves were slaughtered, yet our killings continued.

We were invincible.

During this triumphant time, we picked up a promising new member. His name was Jean Chastel. It wasn't sorrow or misery that drew Françoise to him—it was hatred. Chastel's heart was a burning black coal. His hatred was a perfect match for the Circle, so Françoise appeared to him with an offer. Sign your soul to Moyset, and bring destruction to the world you despise.

Without hesitation, Chastel accepted.

It wasn't until later that we learned Chastel's motive. For years he loved a younger woman. Her name was Jeanne Denis, and she was beautiful. Many months back he approached her with his feelings, and she *laughed* at him! Jeanne's first reaction was Chastel must be joking, that he couldn't possible think they could have a relationship.

After all, Chastel was so *old!* She realized her error soon enough, and apologized for the misunderstanding.

But Chastel never forgot. She *laughed* at him!

Revenge was on his mind as The Gift lifted Chastel from his body. He followed Jeanne's scent to her farmhouse. She was out in the fields, an easy target. The Beast growled to announce itself. Jeanne saw it, a hundred yards away yet with no hope of escape. The monstrosity cleared the field in a manner of seconds.

Chastel's mind was mostly lost to the Beast; these hunting trips are best remembered as a hazy fever dream. But in that moment, a very human thought crossed the Beast's mind.

Who's laughing now, Jeanne?

The Beast pounced, catching her fragile head in its maw. But before he could tear it off, the Beast was struck in the side.

It was Jeanne's younger brother, Jacques Denis, a spear in his hand.

Jacques stabbed the Beast again. Chastel was stunned; he hadn't expected this! The 16 year-old boy used the confusion to make a devastating blow to the Beast's ribcage. Enraged, the Beast retreated to the body of Chastel.

A stupid boy stood between Chastel and

revenge. It was infuriating. And it would not go unpunished.

Jacques Denis would pay. Chastel would make sure of that.

In the weeks to come, Chastel visited the Denis home as a "concerned family friend." The fools bought it. Chastel had to sit through Jacques' retelling of the attack, but the boy painted himself as some kind of hero. Anger burned within Chastel, but he said nothing.

There was good news, however. Jeanne may have survived with only a few marks behind her ears, but her real injuries were of the mind. The experience drove her mad. She uttered nothing but gibberish, and was particularly uneasy when Chastel was near—perhaps sensing the monster within.

Maybe *this* was a better punishment than death.

Jacques left his sister in the care of Margeurite—a young lady from town who he fancied—and took Chastel aside.

"My friend," said Jacques. "The King has sent a renowned hunter to slay *la Bête*. A man by the name of Jean-Charles-Marc-Antoine Vaumesle d'Enneval. They say d'Enneval seeks help from the locals."

"What of it?" barked Chastel, barely

concealing distaste.

Jacques had the eyes of an adult in that moment. "I want to join him. I swear, I *will* kill this Beast, and avenge Jeanne!"

If only Jacques knew the irony of it all. Chastel put an arm on his shoulder. "More power to you, my boy. But please, confide your plans in me first. I wouldn't want you to act rashly, and end up like your sister."

So that's how Chastel became the *Cercle de la Bête's* double-agent.

d'Enneval could not touch us.

Despite his zeal (and the high bounty), the King's hunter failed to stop our onslaught. He saw young Jacques' determination, and they formed an alliance. It was that partnership which betrayed them. Chastel fed their plans back to the Circle. We knew their next move long before they made it.

This was not enough for Chastel. He had another idea, and presented it to Françoise.

"Oh, great Françoise—The Devil's Bride," he pleaded. "Allow me The Gift the day of the spring fair. Let me strike Jacques Denis down in public! Let us make an example of him!"

Françoise listened for the whispers of her Dark Husband. "No," she said at last.

Chastel was shocked. "B—but why not,

my lady?"

"It is too risky. Too many people," Françoise explained. "The Dark Horseman says no."

"I don't understand," said Chastel. "Are we not lords of this land? Do we not tread where we please, fearless of mortals? Is The Gift not strong enough to defeat any who might oppose us at the fair?"

Françoise crossed her arms. "Do you question the word of Moyset?"

"I—well, I..." Chastel shrunk away. "No, my lady. I do not question His word."

They parted ways, but Chastel did not give up so easily.

It is with distaste that I write what follows. For the sake of history I shall record these blasphemies. Let this be a warning to those tempted by disloyalty. For it shall be punished swiftly, and without mercy.

This is from the confessions of Chastel.

Chastel did the unthinkable; he summoned Moyset on his own.

He knew the ritual. Of course he did; we allperformed it every night. But this was heresy. No one but Françoise was permitted to call our Master from the bowels of Hell. She alone had that right, because she is His bride.

But Chastel had no such privilege.

Still, he spoke the words and performed the rite. At its climax, the very moon's light went out; the world was plunged into utter darkness.

And this darkness was not empty.

Chastel felt His presence. How could he not? The air was thick with it, heavy. Chastel felt as if he were underwater. In the deepest, darkest region of the ocean floor. He was panicky, and had the impulse to hold his breath and tread to the surface. Chastel was drowning; he was sure of it. And already he regretted his decision.

Moyset, who was both nowhere and everyone, spoke.

"What heresy is this, mortal?"

Chastel's words caught in his throat. To stand before the Dark Horseman in the flesh is to feel fear and awe distilled together. It creates a singular emotion, so strong as to render the bravest men to their knees.

But there was no turning back. Not now.

"I…" Chastel wet his lips. His tongue was dry as sandpaper. "I have a proposition for you, Master."

"A proposition?"

Chastel nodded.

"I take it thy proposal differs from that which I already declined through my bride?"

One impulse flooded Chastel's mind; run!But even if he dared, where could he flee? This deity was all around him, waiting in every inch of suffocating blackness. He knew there was only one option—beg, and accept whatever fate his Master chose.

"Please, my lord!" Chastel shouted. "I hate this boy, this Jacques Denis! I will serve you forever, be your most loyal servant, if you would only let me kill him!"

Darkness closed in around him. Chastel breathed harder, yet scarcely any oxygen touched his lungs.

"Oh you would, would you? If I abide your wishes now, only then you shall pledge your loyalty?"

Chastel realized his error, too late.

"Thy soul is already mine, heathen. I shall not be threatened with your obedience. If your loyalty is not absolute, then there is only one way out…"

A thousand dark tendrils took Chastel's feet. A scream erupted from his throat. This darkness wasn't just heavy—it was alive, and hungry. These tendrils crawled up his legs, pulling him into the void. Icy hands took hold of Chastel's arms and throat. Absolute, unrelenting terror filled him. He was sure that fear alone would kill him, long before he met whatever abyss was waiting.

"Wait! No, please!" Chastel yelled. "I am yours, my lord! I swear it on my very soul!"

Slowly, they loosened their grip.

"I... I want to spread the fear," said Chastel. "Show the mortals that even in numbers, there is no safety. Not from you, oh great Horseman."

The darkness receded. Chastel could almost breath again.

"Please," he said. "Let me attack at the fair in Malzieu. Let me prove just how unstoppable you are, my lord."

The silence stretched on for ages. Chastel didn't dare move or speak. Silence meant he had a chance.

"A mass slaughter, while the herd is gathered in jovial spirits. Interesting. Mayhap it is worth sacrificing one heathen to observe the outcome of such an assault."

"So... Does that mean you will let me, my lord?" said Chastel.

"Yes."

Chastel gave a sigh of relief.

"But know this, heathen; you still act against my Word. I accept no responsibility for the outcome. When you cease this rampage, you will answer to my bride—and accept whatever punishment she deems fit."

"Y—yes, yes of course!" Chastel could hardly believe it. "Of course, my lord!"

"Now go, my sacrificial lamb. Test thy limits. Stretch thy muscles. And show me just what we are capable

of!"

Suddenly, the darkness converged. It entered through his mouth, choking him. He felt darkness creeping in through his ears, his nostrils, even beneath his fingernails. He squirmed and fought it off, to no avail; he was suffocating. Chastel's limbs went numb. His mind was a blur. He couldn't breathe. Couldn't think. Couldn't even feel.

As Chastel fell, the Beast rose.

At long last, Chastel wore the body of the Beast once again.

It was refreshing. Chastel confessed that only as the Beast did he feel whole. Like this was his true shape, the only form in which his anger could be quenched. The Beast wasted no time—it knew exactly where to go.

The spring fair.

It was the sound of people that drew him. Music. Laughter. Screams of joy. It was beautiful chaos, and the Beast was ready to join in. It stormed the gates of the fair, unafraid. People saw it, screamed, and ran.

None would challenge *la Bête*.

And why would they? Nothing but bodies were left in its wake. Their best attempts to slay it were useless. Even skilled hunters came up empty. Really, what *could* you do, aside from run?

Time to find the boy—Jacques Denis.

The Beast lifted its nose, and caught the scent. It was faint, and not exactly right—but it was close enough. It turned and ran through the fairgrounds.

People spread in a wave as the Beast moved. All the fight these peasants had shown—the hunting parties, the bayonets, the rifles—it was all gone now. They were caught off-guard.

Finally, the Beast tracked the scent to its source. Only, it was not Jacques, but Marguerite. The girl from town who Jacques so fancied.

When Marguerite saw him, she ran like the rest. But she paused longer than most, and really *saw* him. Chastel admitted in that moment, he was convinced that she knew him for what he was. She saw him not as a Beast, but a person. A traitor. A man in wolf's clothing.

She ran not just from the Beast, but from the truth.

The Beast bounded after her. She was no match, of course. The Beast pounced, and tore Marguerite limb from limb.

Chastel confessed that he had two reasons for killing her. One was, of course, the sweet justice of it. She was one of the few things Jacques cherished. Destroying her would hurt the boy in ways that teeth alone never could.

But vengeance was not his biggest reason. It was fear that drove him to rip her apart. He was afraid Marguerite would let out his secret, that he would be the first of the *Cercle de la Bete* to be exposed. So he killed her in a panicked frenzy, hoping to bury his secret with her.

Regardless of reason, it was over now. Marguerite was dead.

But as the Beast killed her, word spread. The villagers grabbed their weapons and steadied their hearts. The element of shock had worn off, and now they were ready to fight.

The Beast was surrounded, but it didn't matter; it caught the boy's scent in the wind.

It charged into the crowd. One foolish man swung at him, but the rest stepped aside. The scent led the Beast outside the fairgrounds. Jacques wasn't at the fair, but was on his way.

The Beast was glad to greet him.

Jacques rode down on his horse, but the Beast blocked the way.

They locked eyes. This foolish, sixteen year-old boy was staring down *la Bête du Gévaudan* for the second time in his short life.

Jacques dismounted, grabbed his spear, and fought.

The length of the spear gave him an advantage. Even with the Beast's powerful legs, it was difficult getting close enough to strike. But Jacques was on the defensive, and growing weak fast. All the Beast had to do was wear him out, then go for the kill.

But just as the boy's vitality wavered, a rifle shot behind them. Surprised, both boy and Beast turned to see the cause.

It was the King's huntsman, d'Enneval.

Behind him were the villagers. They now had weapons, and determination in their eyes. They were ready to fight—to the death if need be. The boy sensed an opportunity, and cut a large gash across his foe.

La Bête was cornered, and couldn't fight them all at once. He had to retreat.

But not before one final glare at the huntsman.

Waves of hatred pulsed through that stare. d'Enneval staggered as if struck by an arrow—which he had. It was an arrow of anger, fury itself shot from the Beast's eye.

The Beast fled.

This is the tale, as Chastel told it. The whole Circle looked upon him, breath held, awaiting Françoise' judgment.

"You disobeyed me," said she. "You

disobeyed me and the Dark Horseman."

"But Françoise!" Chastel pleaded. "Think of the fear! Think of the terror we struck into their hearts!"

Françoise shook her head. "You have proven one thing, Chastel. You cannot be trusted. You are loyal only to your vengeance. You will continue your duties to the Circle, but never again shall you receive The Gift. It is, perhaps... Not safe."

Chastel was devastated. But in the presence of the Devil's Bride, could he argue?

He continued to be our double agent, getting information from the Denis family. Despite the hubris of it, one good thing did come from the spring fair attack—d'Enneval was off the hunt. Jacques begged him to stay, but the hunter was adamant. He was sent to slay a wolf, but those were not the eyes of any such thing.

They were the eyes of a Devil. And that cannot be slain.

d'Enneval was gone. The *Cercle de la Bête* was victorious.

Chapter 4:
Moyset

I put the book down, shaking from head to toe.

There were many empty pages after the story ended. This was a work in progress; the writer must have planned to continue documenting this "Circle of the Beast."

What have I read?

I paced the clearing. My feet couldn't keep up with my racing mind. I wondered what became of them. Why the writing suddenly stopped.

But most of all, I wondered if any of it was true.

Of course, most of it wasn't. It couldn't be. Werewolves, devils... These were all a product of a superstitious past. Before the rise of science, mankind invented all sorts of stories to explain what itdidn't understand.

But this book was not fiction either. That, I was sure of.

So what *really* happened? These transformations were probably the result of natural hallucinogenics. Many plants, if

Chapter 4

used correctly, could induce the feeling of losing yourself. Perhaps even make you believe you became a monster. No doubt Françoisediscovered this, and used her knowledge to appear powerful.

It all made sense. Except, it didn't. Not at all.

What about the villagers? What about the fair? The boy? Had the king really sent one of his best hunters? 1764 was a long time ago, true, but that was also during the French Revolution. A time when science and reason began to overthrow religion. A king in that time would not have set a bounty to kill the *loup-garou* unless they had reason to believe it.

And what of the narrator? If everything else was a hallucination, how do you explain him? He was trampled, never to walk again.

But his legs healed.

That thought pulsed in my mind. I could think of no rational explanation. Even in this age, such a recovery would be unlikely. It was the one thing that escaped me. I could dismiss everything else, be it natural drugs or superstitious manipulation.

But his legs healed!

I paced, faster and faster. The moon was nearly as bright as day. It illuminated everything—except the answer to that one question; how?

If the narrator's legs really did heal, what else was true? Could there have been some kind of Beast? Was there really a Dark Horseman, who could perform miracles?

If so, could He... Could he save Eleanor?

I slapped myself hard across the face. "Get a hold of yourself, Connor," I said. After the day I had, I allowed myself irrational thoughts. And can you blame me? Between the locals of Mende, my unnerving visit with Dr. DuPuis, getting lost in the woods, and now reading an ancient book about werewolves? Of course I was on edge! But the stinging slap was a reality check. There was nothing to it. No Beast. No Devil. No miracles.

But his legs healed!

Still that thought made me doubt everything. I couldn't explain it away, as much as I tried.

Hesitantly, I picked up the book, and thumbed to the page with the summoning rite. I squinted at the writing—it was an old French dialect that was slow to translate.

On an impulse, I took a pen from my pocket and wrote my own translation on the back of the page.

Had you asked me then, I couldn't have told you why I did it. Why I turned that ritual into something I could read, remember, and perhaps even speak. Looking back, I know exactly why; I was a man at the end of the line. This was it. After searching the entire globe, all I came to was this. Nothing would happen. I knew that, deep down. But this was the last stone left unturned, and I intended to turn it.

Because if I didn't, I had to admit it was over.

I looked at my handwriting, normally so neat, and saw nothing but chicken scratch. But there they were; the words in English, as best as I could translate. I read them over and over, and realized what I had to do.

I would perform this ritual. It was foolish. It was stupid.

But at least then I could say I tried everything.

"Shiver! Shiver! Shiver!

"Come! Come! Come!"

The words echoed in the quiet night. I stood in the center of the circle, just like the one in the book, and spoke the whole thing.

One last step.

Chapter 4

With a pocketknife I made an incision across my arm. The blood dripped into a small bowl of water. I did it. As I held a handkerchief to my wound, I wondered... Now what?

The forest was completely still. With each silent second, any irrational hope faded.

It's over. All over.

I bent over on the spot, and cried like I never cried before. Perhaps only when completely alone can you fall apart so completely. I was overcome with deep, agonizing sobs, each more heart-wrenching than the last.

I failed. I would go home to a grave.

Part of me didn't even want to go back. Eleanor didn't recognize me, anyway. I could lay here in the forest, until the wilderness swallowed me whole.

That's when the silence was broken.

It was the unmistakable howl of a wolf. The hair all across my body shot up. I felt electrocuted! Unnerved didn't begin to describe the adrenaline pumping through my body. That howl was close. Too close.

Then I saw it; a wolf emerged from the woods.

As far as I could tell, this was no monster. Just a mundane breed of wolf. But it didn't have to be—this was a real and perfectly earthly danger.

Panicking, I racked my brain for any factoid of wolf survival. Over the years, I must have heard *something* pertaining to wolf attacks. I had the vaguest sense that I had, although the details eluded me. The best I could think of was not to make sudden movements and never, ever make eye contact. Was it wolves that considered eye contact a threat? I wasn't sure, but it was my best bet.

None of it mattered, anyway. Because I then heard a sound so chilling, it could not be of this world.

"As I hath been summoned, here I present myself."

The voice was unlike anything I had heard. It was

somehow... Reptilian, although I couldn't say what made me think that. It was raspy, uneven, yet crystal clear. Not a single word was misunderstood.

Breath caught in my throat. Where was this voice? Did it come from the wolf? Was that even possible?

The voice seemed to come from everywhere. No, that's not right... It was coming from nowhere. Nowhere and everywhere.

A long silence followed. I started to wonder if I had imagined the whole thing. Maybe the wolf wasn't even real. Was this all some hallucination? Have I driven myself insane with grief?

Just as I started to believe that, I heard it again.

"What is thy reason for rousing me?"

I chanced a peek at the wolf. It was standing there, staring right at me. I didn't meet its gaze—I knew *that* would be the end of me—but I knew it was staring.

This voice... It was not real. Couldn't be. One word came up from my panic-stricken mind—schizophrenia. Fear and sorrow broke my sanity, and now I heard voices that didn't exist.

If only that was true.

"Human!" The voice boomed. The force of it knocked me off my feet. *"You hath woken me from the slumber of eons. Now speak thy reason, or feel my wrath!"*

The wolf snarled, matching the anger of the voice. It was poised, ready to pounce any moment.

Finally, everything came crashing down. Eleanor was gone. And I was not far behind. I was going to die a madman, eaten by wolves while hearing voices in my head.

No point resisting now.

"I came to save my wife," I whimpered.

Another long silence. Then, finally, the voice returned. *"It is matters of the heart which brought you here? How*

Chapter 4

quaint. But how strong is thy resolve? To what lengths would you go for the salvation of thy bride?"

"I would do anything!" I shouted. I hated the sound of myself, so weak and defeated.

"Anything? Even at the cost of thy life?"

"Of course!"

"Even at the expense of thy soul?"

"I... Yes, even that."

"Look at me, human." The voice was a gentle purr, seductively sweet. I let my eyes fall on the wolf. It stood calm, but its eyes... They were too bright, and somehow seemed wrong. They were not a wolf's eyes at all. They were something different, something unknown.

"I can save her."

Although the wolf didn't move, I knew it was connected. It was some kind of messenger, a representative of Moyset Himself.

"Wh—what do I have to do?" I asked.

Alien laughter cackled through the woods.

"You read the book, did you not? You know the nature of this bargain."

It felt like there was a rock in my throat. The words struggled to come out. "I... I become a werewolf. A *loup-garou.* And then she'll get better. Right?" I pleaded. "Please, tell me she'll get better!"

"Oh, she will get better. This illness of the mind, which you so dread, shall be lifted."

For the first time since I came to France, I felt a flicker of real hope.

"Is it possible?" I asked.

"Yes... But nothing is without a price. Your soul for hers. You shall become my body, and thy soul the chariot of my wishes."

I was not a complete fool. I wanted to know what I was agreeing to. "Tell me, will I still be able to see her? To

Moyset

hold her, kiss her, and love her?"

"Yes. The days shall be yours together, to live in matrimony. But your nights... Those belong to me."

If I were in my right mind, I would have seen the horror of this bargain. But my mind was anything but right. Please, try not to judge me. Can a man be condemned for a decision made at his weakest moment? When a man drowns at sea, can you expect him to discriminate if it's friend or foe who offers salvation?

This was the greatest mistake of my life. That's obvious now. But if you had gone through what I went through, been consumed by grief and terrified by fear... Would you really have the strength to refuse?

I didn't just say the words. I believed them. My heart and soul accepted it as true.

"I am yours, Moyset."

The wolf stepped closer. Now, I realized what was wrong with its eyes. I knew them. They were yellow instead of blue, but there was no mistaking it.

They were my eyes.

The wolf pounced.

What followed was a lunatic's dream. At least, that's how it felt.

Everything was so vivid. I saw each brushstroke of the world around me, down to the smallest blade of grass. The subtlest sounds filled my ears with unfathomable depths and detail.

Most intense of all was the smell.

I was overwhelmed by it. Millions—no, *billions*—of unique aromas dominated my senses. None were repulsive. Even the foulest scents were fascinating.

Many hours later, I awoke next to the river outside of

Chapter 4

town. I had only the vaguest memories of what transpired.

I remembered the forest, lit up by dazzling new eyes.

I remembered running. Running faster than possible.

And I remembered the hunger, burning within me.

But that was all. Everything else was a hazy cloud of raw emotions, full of passion but lacking detail.

I glanced at my reflection in the water. My hair was tangled. My clothes torn. My body covered in dirt and grime. I was a mess.

And I was different. I could feel it.

Had I become a werewolf? Maybe. Maybe not. But one thing was for sure; my business in France was finished. That very day I packed my bags, and began my journey back to the States.

I was returning home. But I wasn't coming back alone.

Chapter 5:
The Halloween Hunt

I returned from France with a demon on my back.

The trip gave me too much time to think. I brooded over what happened on that mountain. During that time, I came to accept a hard truth.

It was real. All of it.

I couldn't explain how, of course. It went against everything I believed. But Moyset was real. I could feel Him, even now. There was a weight on my shoulders, and a shadow over my heart.

I was a changed man.

Now, I could only hope it was worth it.

It was the middle of the night when I finally arrived in Elkhorn.

Barbason greeted me at the door. He saw how shaken I was, and asked, "Did ye find what ye was lookin' for over there?"

Chapter 5

I couldn't tell him. For me to believe it was one thing, but to say it out loud? I wasn't ready for that.

"It's been taken care of," I said. My brother wasn't convinced, but said nothing.

Then came the moment I was waiting for.

I crept up the stairs, and into the dark bedroom to see my wife.

Eleanor was fast asleep. Already my eyes stung with tears. I had missed her so much. Her hair was disheveled. She probably forgot to comb it before bed, as she always did. She started forgetting before I left, but I took care of it if she didn't. Barbason, despite his best intentions, couldn't know all the little nuances that made Eleanor who she was. Not like I could. After all these years, I knew her completely.

Gently, I stroked the hair from her face. I managed to get it somewhat straightened, and she looked almost like herself again.

I leaned down, and kissed the love of my life. A tear drop fell next to where my lips touched. I backed out of the room, as quietly as I entered.

She never even knew I was there.

But maybe, just maybe, she will soon.

These October nights were chillier than ever.

I hardly slept anymore. I spent my days exhausted and my nights terrified. There was always a presence inside of me, squirming around the pit of my stomach.

At night I heard Him whispering. Unintelligible ramble, most of the time. Syllables that made no coherent words, but were frightening all the same. I tried to ignore it, but couldn't—it was a constant buzzing in my ear.

I was becoming an insomniac.

And things were worse than ever for Eleanor. She

was so different. All of the vigor that defined her was gone. And I still had to remind her who I was.

Two nights after my return, I dozed off in my recliner. But the moment my mind slipped from consciousness, it was taken somewhere horrible.

"'Tis night, tis night and the devil's light
"Cast glimmering beams around!"
A huge bonfire. A circle of savages dance. Their hair matted. Eyes wild. Teeth sharp.
"The maras dance, the nisses prance
"On the flower-enamelled ground."
A woman wore a wolf skin. Walks to the fire.
"'Tis night! 'tis night! and the werewolf's might
"Makes man and nature shiver."
Chanting louder. Faster. The flames glow blue. Cold.
"To the great Moyset, I have this to say;
"Thy presence please deliver!"
Eyes. Ruthless, menacing. Eyes in the fire. Eyes staring. Staring.
Staring at me.

I awoke with a gasp. My heart pounded against my ribcage. It took several seconds just to realize where I was.

That wasn't just a dream. It was a memory. The Circle of the Beast at its prime. Moyset wanted me to see it. He wanted me to remember that I belong to Him.

It was Halloween, and I had barely slept.

Insomnia was awful, but I couldn't bear to think about the alternative. I didn't trust myself alone. I especially didn't trust myself asleep.

Apparently Barbason didn't trust me, either. He

Chapter 5

visited more in the weeks since my return than in years before. He noticed the change in me. I couldn't hide the dark rings around my eyes, or the sickly pallor of my skin. My mind was clouded by nonsensical babble.

"Ye need a doctor," Barbason told me.

"I am a doctor," I replied. I needed him to leave. He was growing suspicious, and I was becoming paranoid. What if he discovered the truth?

He crossed his arms. "Ye know what I mean. Ye ain't well, Connor. Keep up like this, and ye'll wither away faster than Eleanor."

Withering away. Is that what was happening?

"I'll call someone soon," I said. It was a lie, and I think he knew it, but it closed the topic for now.

Meanwhile, one word kept rising from the demon's ramble.

Hunt. Hunt. Hunt.

Before long, it was all I could hear. My brother left, and the silent house was filled by this mantra.

Then, all of a sudden, it stopped.

The silence was worse. I knew it meant something. I held my breath, waiting for something to happen.

"Remember our deal, mortal."

It was the voice of Moyset in its full, dominant timbre.

"Your soul, for hers."

I glanced at Eleanor, fast asleep by five o' clock. I quietly closed the door, and went to the empty living room.

"Fine," said I, opening my arms. "Do what you must with me."

Then I fell into a deep, deep sleep.

What happened next was utterly surreal, like a dream

The Halloween Hunt

with more substance.

I remember looking down at myself, lying on the floor. It was an out-of-body experience. I wasn't so much weightless as buoyant. The air was like water, and I was swimming with the ease of a fish.

It's important you understand one thing; I was not myself.

I was seeing and feeling it all. But it was not me in control. It was Moyset. He was possessing me, and I was just a passenger in my own mind.

Everything the Beast did was Him, not me. I cannot be held responsible.

Can I?

Regardless, my mind (or spirit, or astral projection—whatever this was) left the house, and flew through the sky. I could hear the Beast's thoughts, which were primal and terrifying. It saw the world in black and white. Friend, or enemy.

Predator... Or prey.

And the Beast's thoughts revolved around one thing; *Barbason knows.* It knew my brother's suspicion would lead him to the truth. The Beast was threatened, like an animal backed into a corner.

So what does a cornered wolf do?

It fights.

I flew to the outskirts of town. Finally, I descended upon my brother's home. B.R. Amon & Sons, inc., where only one son ever worked.

With incredible ears, I heard the patter of footsteps on the pavement. Immature voices. Laughter.

Children.

A girl in the house next door waved goodbye to her friends. She almost went home, but instead crossed the parking lot to B.R. Amon and knocked.

Chapter 5

My brother *(Traitor. Enemy. Prey)* answered the door. The girl said "Trick or treat" and held out a bag. Barbason searched for some kind of candy. His home was not on many kids' trick-or-treating route. He found some packaged sweet, and gave it to the girl.

The Beast's attention drifted from Barbason to the girl.

She was so *vibrant!* I can't explain it. There was an aura around her, glowing in the twilight. The Beast knew what this light was, even if I didn't.

It was life. Energy.

Prey.

I realized that *this* was what the Beast needed. Not flesh, no... That was just a means to get to this. This vital energy was the Beast's diet.

It watched her, trying to decide if it could take her down. Devour her for her radiance. I became aware of how hungry I was. Not in my stomach, no. I was hungry in the soul. Hungry for this.

Then the girl saw me. *Really* saw me.

Our eyes met. Mine filled with hunger. Hers with terror. I had no idea *what* she saw; as far as I knew, I was an incorporeal being. A ghost, or something similar. But judging from the look in her eye, she must have seen what the farmers described in *Livre de la Bête*.

She saw the Beast of Gévaudan.

But, luckily for her, the Beast was still weak. It didn't have the strength to slay such big game. No, best to start small, and come back for her later.

The Beast vanished, and flew into the wind.

That night, thewoods around Elkhorn became my hunting ground.

The Halloween Hunt

There was no shortage of prey; no squirrel, raccoon, or possum was safe. The Beast hunted, gradually sating its hunger. The animals' bodies were torn apart, but it was that vital essence which the Beast consumed. I found that *all* living creatures had that aura, not just the girl. Sure, the life force from a raccoon wasn't nearly so bright, but it would do.

Were all humans as vibrant as her? Or was she special?

Again, I must remind you; I was only a spectator in all this. I had no control of myself, and was forced to witness these nightmares unfold.

The Beast was the apex predator of the woods. As it got stronger, it also got bolder. It hunted closer to human land, and didn't shy away when caught in the headlights of an approaching car. It stared down the driver, making one thing very clear...

This was the Beast's territory now.

Many hours later, I returned home.

My mind and body were conflicted. My mind knew I should feel terrible; I was out all night, hunting and feasting on raw meat. I should be exhausted. I should be sick.

But it was quite the opposite.

I felt rejuvenated. Alive like I hadn't been in months. I tested myself, walking through the house. There was a new spring in my step. Vigor in my blood. It was as if somehow...

The thought stopped me dead in my tracks.

I knew *exactly* where all this energy came from, and it wasn't a good night's rest. It was life. The life force of all those creatures the Beast slaughtered. I had been refreshed by their deaths.

Shame and excitement boiled inside of me. I tried not to think about it, and go about my day normally. But I

Chapter 5

couldn't ignore the feeling of fullness. I couldn't forget where it came from.

And I had to admit, it felt great.

In the following weeks, miracles started to happen.

It was dinner time, and I had some of Eleanor's favorites; steak, mashed potatoes, green beans. I had to cut it all into bite-size pieces, of course, and fed it to her myself. She kept mostly to her bed now, her motor skills quickly deteriorating. This had become our routine, and she always ate with a zombie-like submission. No emotion, no joy. Like eating on auto-pilot.

Not tonight.

I fed that first piece of steak into her mouth, and something changed. For the first time in months, her blues eyes stared right into mine. I knew that look—I would know it anywhere! That was my wife, Eleanor Amon. Her eyes smiled, even if her lips couldn't.

She was really *tasting* it!

Eleanor gratefully took the next piece of steak, and finished her meal with enthusiasm. After dinner I kissed her goodnight, and she looked right into me again. Sharp, alert eyes. The eyes of the girl I fell in love with more than half a century ago. That girl was still in there. This disease didn't destroy her, not yet.

Once alone, I nearly cried with joy.

I hope you never experience what I did. I hope you never have to watch someone you love so deeply lose themselves like that. It's a slow, torturous process. But if you do, you'll understand how one single look can cause such happiness.

Then, a thought froze me in place.

She's living on stolen lives.

The Halloween Hunt

This is what the Beast was hunting for. Not just for Moyset, and not just for me. It was slaying living creatures, and sending some of that energy back to Eleanor.

Should I still be grateful?

I suppose I should. After all, they were only animals. Was meat gathered by tooth and claw any different than meat served on a plate? I would exchange the lives of countless small creatures for Eleanor's health. Maybe that's morbid, but it's the simple truth. And I suspect you would say the same in my position.

But there was that twisted voice at the base of my spine. That otherworldly babble. Its appetite was only growing. I knew it was a only matter of time before it wanted more than small game.

Then I remembered the girl.

I remembered how energy pulsed from her. I remembered how full, and vibrant, and alive it was. And I remembered how the Beast hungered for her. I think that's when I knew what this would come to. I knew the demon inside of me wouldn't be content with squirrels for long. That was just the appetizer as it built its strength. Then, it would go after the *real* target. I almost lost my dinner as the thought sunk in.

I was going to hunt and kill humans.

Memories from the Book of the Beast flooded back. Hunting parties. Men with rifles and pitchforks. Bodies mutilated. Villages preparing for battle.

I imagined Elkhorn at arms. My friends and neighbors with shotguns and spears. I could see them surrounding my home, storming down the door, taking me alive or dead.

Perhaps that mental image was too medieval, but perhaps not. After all, isn't this a medieval situation? A werewolf, hidden in town, slaying his brothers and sisters.

Chapter 5

Such a primal threat might cause a primal reaction. People might lose their civility, become no more than animals themselves.

What's the rule of survival for weaker animals?

Strength in numbers.

Could they sense it in me? I always felt the presence of Moyset. The shadow of the Beast hung over me at all times. But could others feel it too? And if they didn't now, would they later? As the Beast gets stronger, will I become more a monster myself? Will people instinctively shy away, sensing the predator among them? Would I be hanged? Burned at the stake?

I couldn't escape these thoughts, but I reminded myself; Eleanor is getting better.

Was it worth it?

Did I care if this village hated me? As long as I had my wife, perhaps it didn't matter if I was an outcast. So I kept my end of the bargain, just as Moyset was keeping His.

Every day, Eleanor got better. And the Beast got hungrier.

Before long, Eleanor was having whole conversations with me. Scattered memories returned. Everyone was amazed. It was a miracle! Everyone toasted to her good health.

Except for me.

I sank away from the celebrations, and hardly remarked at their joy. I knew the dark secret; the final breaths of a hundred slaughtered animals filled her lungs, and their blood beat in her heart.

Eleanor was animated by death. And I was its bringer.

I tried to remember the terms of our agreement. When she healed, would I be free? I didn't think so. I started to suspect that she would keep getting better, and I would only get worse.

I was so full of guilt, I could hardly look at her.

Every time I did, I was reminded of what I was becoming. I didn't know what to do. I needed help. I desperately needed a second opinion.

I had to tell someone. And I knew only one person I could trust with something so insane.

Barbason.

Chapter 6:
A Devil's Bargain

"Brother, I need to tell you something. But you've got to promise it stays between us. No matter how ill you think of me, you can't speak of this."

Barbason looked puzzled. "O' course, Connor. What's botherin' ye?"

How to even begin?

"I... I found something while in France," I told him. "Something that could save Eleanor. But at a price. A steep, steep price."

Barbason crossed his arms and gave me an appraising look. "What was it?"

"This," I said.

Livre de la Bête fell onto the table. A cloud of dust erupted around its edges, making it appear grainy—like something out of an old movie.

I brought the book back with me from France, although it never left my suitcase. The only reason I brought it out now was evidence; without *something* to show for my claims, would anyone believe me? Sure, it was all in French and my brother couldn't read it, but maybe he too would get that creeping sensation around it. Maybe it was just enough to make such a nightmarish story seem possible.

Barbason stared at it. "That ain't no medical textbook."

"No," I said. My words were hollow. Dazed, even. "It's not. It belonged to a cult of demon worshipers. Moyset, that was the demon's name. Moyset, the Devil's Messenger. These pages speak of miracles to those loyal to Him. Dark ones, no doubt, but miracles all the same. There's an incantation to call this demon."

I looked at my brother. Did he believe me? Or think I'm crazy? His face wouldn't tell. I forced myself to keep talking.

"I tried it, and... It worked. Moyset came. It was the most terrifying experience of my life. He came, and said that He could cure her of CJD. But, in return, He wanted the one thing He didn't have—a body. My body."

Barbason's eyebrow went up, no more than half an inch. "So ye're telling me ye're possessed?"

I took a deep breath. This wouldn't be easy.

"No," I said. "I'm telling you I'm a werewolf."

The word hung in the air like the cloud of dust. I never imagined such words would come from my mouth. It was silly, and ridiculous... But true. Barbason studied my face, looking for a sign that this was some kind of joke. All he saw was my ashen face, and perhaps a devilish tint to my eyes.

He took a seat beside me, and put his arm around my shoulder. He believed. Barbason wasn't smart, but at that moment I thanked God for having him. He believed, and now I wasn't carrying this burden alone. The simple act of telling someone was a great relief.

"So, that's how Eleanor be gettin' better? Some sort

Chapter 6

o' Devil's bargain?" said Barbason.

A Devil's bargain. Yes, that was exactly it. I nodded. He caught the gist of my situation in two simple words. I was stuck in a Devil's bargain.

"Where'd ye even get this book?" he asked. "Not exactly what I thought ye'd be lookin' for. Did that doctor give it to ye?"

I didn't answer him. I *couldn't*. Telling him about Moyset was hard, but it had to be done. But to speak of the insanity at Dr. DuPuis' clinic...

It was more than I could bear.

Thankfully, my brother let it go.

"So, Eleanor's been gettin' better and ye're... What, exactly?" Barbason looked into my troubled eyes. "What have ye been doin', Connor?"

I closed my eyes, collecting my thoughts. "At night, I change. This demon takes over, and I become a monster. And I hunt. So far, it's only been small animals, but... The Beast is getting hungrier."

Barbason rubbed a hand across his face. "Ye know, people 'round town been seein' something strange. Some kind o' big dog or wolf. Folks been callin' it the Beast o' Bray Road. It's ye, isn't it?"

I gave a pained nod.

"Ye know, ain't no good ever come o' these kind o' bargains," Barbason said. He tried to be gentle, but there was no mistaking the reprimand in his voice. "Does more harm than good."

"I know," I said. "I know it was a mistake, that I shouldn't have done it. But I wasn't thinking clearly. Now that I am, I don't know how to get out." My voice got increasingly desperate. I grabbed my brother by the collar. "I want out, Barbason! *I want out!*"

I shook him with each word, then collapsed into his

A Devil's Bargain

chest. All I could do was sob. Barbason didn't know how to comfort me, so he patted me on the back and said, "I don't know nothin' about the devil. But if there's anythin' I can do to help, ye just let me know."

"Thank you," I said. "Thank you, my brother."

Every day I repeated the words. *I want out. I want out. I want out.*

And all the while, Eleanor got better. In fact, not long after my conversation with Barbason, she requested Chinese food!

That might not sound like much, not to you. But compared to the drone-like attitude she had not long ago, it was miraculous. I ordered everything off the menu and had it delivered. Eleanor had an entire buffet, right in our kitchen.

As we ate, a horrible knot clenched in my stomach.

Is she going to know? Is she going to find out my secret?

And, if she does... Will she hate me for it?

That thought never occurred to me. My focus was always on her recovery; I didn't wonder what she would think of her treatment. Maybe, as she gets more aware, she will see something foreign in her husband. A darkness that wasn't there before.

What if she's disgusted by what I've done?

I want out. I want out. Out. Out! OUT!

Once both of us were full, we had our fortune cookies. I helped Eleanor read hers. It said, *"You will soon get a surprise from a loved one."* It made her smile.

I opened mine, and felt my blood turn to ice.

The fortune said, *"She's not safe yet."*

Eleanor asked what was wrong, but I couldn't speak. Could hardly even breath. As soon as I regained some

Chapter 6

composure, I excused myself and went to the living room to think.

I was *terrified.* Every little hair on my arms, legs, and the back of my neck stood up. My heart pounded against my ribcage, a steady *thump-thump, thump-thump* so strong it hurt.

And it got worse.

"You didn't really think it'd be that easy, did you?" said a voice from behind me.

I literally jumped. I was alone in the house, aside from Eleanor. Or at least, I thought I was. I turned around to see an empty living room.

Where have I heard that voice before?

It was oddly familiar, but I couldn't place it. Not Eleanor's, and thankfully not the raspy voice I heard in the woods.

"Wh—who's there?" I called.

A pause. Then, "It's your conscience, Connor."

That's when it hit me; of course I knew that voice. It was my own.

I tried to pinpoint where it came from. My eyes went to an old family portrait. I had my arm around a much younger Eleanor, holding baby Cassandra. Eleanor smiled and Cassandra giggled. But my face had none of the carefree joy I remembered. No, my portrait was staring straight out at me.

Then I saw my picture's lips move as it spoke. "Trying to back out of the deal already? My, my, and I had such high hopes for you, Connor."

Thump-thump, thump-thump, thump-thump. My heart hammered away. I was probably on the verge of a heart attack; fear itself finally killing me. I was lightheaded, and trembling from head to toe.

"No," I whispered. "This... Isn't real. I'm hallucinating. That's all."

A Devil's Bargain

The portrait grinned. "That tired old excuse again? Please." It winked at me. "Insanity might hold up in court, but not here. You know better. It's all too real."

I shook my head violently. "No!" I shouted. "I didn't believe it—any of it! This is nonsense. I'm a man of science, for God's sake!"

The picture laughed. It was shrill, and humorless. "Not anymore. You are neither a man of science, nor a man of God. Now, you belong only to me."

That's when I knew. It wasn't His voice and it wasn't His body. It probably *was* a hallucination, but that didn't matter; these were His words, just with a different messenger.

This was Moyset.

"And I don't appreciate your disloyalty, doctor," said the picture. "Perhaps you need a reminder of who pulls the strings."

Slowly my picture's young hand slid around Eleanor's shoulder, up her collarbone, and grasped her throat. Her picture still smiled, as if nothing was wrong. But my picture now had a killer's glint in its eyes.

"She's not safe yet. And remember; I can destroy more easily than I can cure."

"But—no!" I reached toward the picture, as if there was something I could do. "You can't! Our deal, remember? You promised to save her! You promised that she would be spared!"

"Spared?" said the picture. "Oh dear Connor, no. I never promised to *spare* her. I simply said I would free her from this disease. I never promised how long she would last afterward. That part is up to *my* discretion."

The hand tightened around Eleanor's throat. Her face became gaunt and white. What was once a laugh became a silent scream.

"You will do my bidding, Connor. Do it to the letter.

Chapter 6

And if you so much as think about betraying me... Then I will take from you the only thing that's ever mattered."

"Stop it!" I yelled. "Please, stop!"

"Time to prove your loyalty, Connor." My portrait sounded as if it were holding back laughter.

"I—I'll do it," I said. "Whatever it is, I'll do it. I'll do anything."

I know, I know; those are dangerous words. The same words that got me into this trap. But what else could I do? I was beyond escape. If I didn't cooperate, Moyset would take my wife and continue to control me. I really didn't have a choice at all.

The picture smiled. "Good. Then you must silence the only other person who knows; your brother. Kill Barbason. Prove how much you are willing to give. Do that, and I'll let her live."

The hands loosened around Eleanor's neck. Her picture returned to normal.

Numbness covered me. I was defeated. All I could do was nod, and obey my master's wishes.

"Good," said the picture. "Now run along, doctor. You don't want to see how long my patience lasts."

Chapter 7:
Heart Stopper

The next night, I invited Barbason over.

I gave him a believable reason; I said I needed company. Of course he believed it. Why wouldn't he? He alone knew what I was struggling with. He was the only personI could turn for comfort.

Tonight, his presence was far from comforting.

It was well after dark. Barbason had dinner with us, and now Eleanor was fast asleep. So we sat in front of the warm fireplace, a bottle of beer in our hands.

"She's gettin' better," he said. I couldn't tell if I was being scolded or not.

I took a deep drink from my beer, and nodded.

"And how are ye doin', Connor?" Barbason asked.

Worse than you know, I thought. He had no clue how deep my anxiety ran. I didn't even pretend to nod. We sat in silence, watching the flames dance across the hearth. Once both of our bottles were empty, I stood up.

"Another one?" I asked.

Chapter 7

As I turned toward the kitchen, a sick thought crossed my mind.

Kill him...

The empty glass bottle was in my hand. I had a clear shot at the back of his head. Without even realizing it, I lifted the bottle high above him. It would either knock him out, or shatter into a sharper weapon. It could all be over before he knew what happened.

Do it...

But I couldn't. I knew Eleanor's life was on the line, but I couldn't bring myself to murder my brother in cold blood. Defeated, I went to the kitchen for more beer.

I dropped the bottles in the recycling bin, then went for the fridge. But something caught my eye on the counter—the knife block.

Ignoring the drinks, I took out and examined each knife. They were all of varying lengths and thicknesses. Each one designed to cut a specific target.

Which one to cut flesh? I thought.

Nothing serrated, no. That you had to slowly cut back and forth, like carving a turkey. No, that would not do. The parring knife was quick and sharp, but wouldn't penetrate deep enough. I needed to strike a major organ. Slice open his lungs or stomach, and he'd be in too much pain to respond. Incapacitated until death. That's what I needed. I found just such a knife. Built to fillet large fish, it was razor sharp and maybe 6 inches long. I could sneak up behind him, slit his throat, and watch him silently bleed out.

What am I saying? This was madness!

I threw the knife back, a little too quickly. Nerves buzzing, I brought the beers back to the living room. I handed Barbason his, and we continued to watch the fire in silence.

The embers grew dim. I got up, took the poker, and

prodded the firewood. As I did, I noticed how wonderfully heavy the iron poker was. Excellent to bludgeon with. One hard knock across the skull, and he'd be out for good.

The brain is fragile, after all. A neurologist would know. I was transfixed by the end of the poker. It turned orange from heat.

I gasped when a hand touched my shoulder.

"We'll get through this," said Barbason. "I know it don't seem like it now, but we'll find a way. Ye just gotta be strong, Connor."

How ironic. He came to comfort me, not knowing I was plotting his demise. I heard the words, but my mind was still on the poker. How sizzling hot it must be. All I had to do was swing it, right now, and it'd all be over.

Do it...

"No..." I said. "No, I can't! I can't do it!"

My poor brother must have thought I was talking about Eleanor. He massaged my shoulder, which was balled up in a knot.

Do it... Or else.

"I... I can't," I said.

Do it...

"No!"

DO IT!

"I can't do it!"

The red-hot poker fell to the floor. And so did I—collapsed to my knees, tears flowing down my face.

"I can't do it..." I sobbed.

Barbason knelt beside me. "There, there. We just gotta hang in there a little longer. There, there."

But as he comforted me, the voice slithered back into my head.

Very well... Your choice has been made.

Chapter 7

As soon as my brother closed the door, my internal battle began.

The Beast tore at my soul. I felt as if there was a hook latched onto my gut. And at the other end, this demon reeled me in.

I had to resist. Had to fight. I pulled back with all my might.

"No!" I said. "You can't do this! I'll do anything, I'll—"

"Anything?"

It was His voice. Not just his words in my mind, but the true voice of Moyset Himself. Every little corner of the room echoed with it.

"Anything, you say? You would do... Anything?"

I shivered. Suddenly I was very cold and nauseous.

"Anything except that which I commanded. 'Slay thy brother,' I said. 'Slay the one who knows the truth.' But this, you did not. You hath failed me, human. Failed my orders. Now... Thou shalt suffer the consequences!"

A gale of wind ripped through the house. Windows flew open. Pictures fell from the mantel. I was buffeted off my feet, my hair flying in a wild tangle.

The wind was all blowing up the stairs.

I knew what He was going to do.

"You can't take Eleanor!" I shouted. I sprang to my feet and ran with the current upstairs. "You'll have to kill me before I'll let you take her!"

My feet soared up the stairs, skipping every other step. The wind was fierce and earsplitting. I turned for the bedroom door. It flew open as I approached, knocked from its hinges by the wind.

"I will stop you!" I growled. All of my emotions—anger, fear, frustration—all melded into one. I was lost within them. I bounded through the door frame, my feet hardly touching the ground. I felt stronger than I have in ages. Maybe, just maybe, I could stop this demon in time.

A dark shadow lurked over my wife's side of the bed.

It was Him. It had to be.

Instinctively, I pounced at Him. I seemed to cross the distance of the room in a single bound. I charged into the demon, and felt myself go *inside* of Him. It was a reversal of roles; now, it was I who possessed Moyset.

I crawled through his infernal veins, until I found the source—His heart. With all the power I had, I clenched the fiend's heart. I was strangling the life out of it, the damnable thing beating slower and slower until it barely pulsed at all.

I did it! I was victorious. I did the impossible, and defeated the demon.

But my celebration was cut short.

"C—Connor...?"

The voice was feeble, barely a whisper. It was the dying breath of a voice I knew all too well.

I heard the *thump* of a body hit the floor. I looked down and realized the shadow wasn't Moyset.

It was Eleanor.

And I wasn't myself. Without realizing it I had shifted into the incorporeal body of the Beast.

I gave an agonized howl, and shot back to my body as fast as I could. There it lay, unconscious on the floor below. I returned with a jolt, stood up, and rushed back upstairs. My body felt like lead.

When I got to the bedroom, I ran to the bed.

Held my wife.

Cradled her.

Kissed her.

But it was too late.

Eleanor Amon—the one love of my life—was gone.

Chapter 8:
What Would Eleanor Do?

Saturday, December 19th.

That was the day I buried my wife.

Everything since her death was a blur. I moved through each day as if I were walking through water. It was all in slow motion. I was drifting—yes, that's the word for it. Drifting through life.

It was declared a heart attack. That was true, in an ironic way. I couldn't stand to look myself in the eye. I couldn't look *anybody* in the eye. I flinched away from my own reflection.

But today, I would have to look at my wife. One last time.

Everyone made it for Eleanor's funeral. Friends from far and wide. Old colleagues of mine. Our daughter and her family came up from Beloit. Will, my poor grandson, looked lost. I bet he had never been to a funeral before. Clearly he didn't know how he was supposed to act.

Frankly, neither did I.

What Would Eleanor Do?

I kept my distance from the casket. I knew that if I approached—*when* I approached, for surely I'd have to—I would fall apart. I wasn't ready for that. So I received hugs from old friends who no longer mattered, and got blessings and best wishes from more people than I could count. I nodded at them, but didn't hear a word of it. For my mind could only think about one thing.

I killed her.

After all of this, she still died. And it was by my hand.

Barbason pulled me aside, so we could speak in private.

"This was no heart attack, was it?" he asked.

I couldn't bring myself to speak. He took my silence for an answer.

"So, what's that mean for ye? Is yer demon still there?" Barbason said.

The insane babbling still rang in my ears. Although now, it almost sounded like laughter.

"He still has me," I said.

Barbason didn't know what to say. He took me in his arms and hugged me tight. "We'll get through this, Connor. I know it don' seem like it now, but ye can still beat this demon, and get yer life back.

"What about Eleanor?" I said. "Can anything get her life back now?"

Barbason's expression fell. "No, I s'pose not. But would she really want ye to fall apart? It might be too late for her, but it ain't too late for ye."

My brother's speech sounded great. But I had no ambition left. No fight in me. *Eleanor* was my strength. I would do anything for her. But, when it mattered the most, I failed. I killed her.

Dr. DuPuis was right; I was becoming an empty husk. Too weak to live. Too weak even to die. I would live out my

Chapter 8

days as a monster.

I hated it all, but what could I do?

Barbason saw his words fell on deaf ears. He gave one last reassuring squeeze, then let me be.

Finally, I went up to the casket.

At the sight of her body, I broke down. No real words came out. Just a painful stream of tears.

She was gone. Gone forever. And I was completely alone.

In the following days, I became more Beast than man.

I actually looked forward to the change. When Moyset took over, I didn't think about her as much. I was simply a monster; hunting, feeding, and growing stronger.

Why fight it when there was nothing left to fight for?

Christmas approached. My daughter invited me to spend the holiday with her family. Barbason extended a similar offer. I refused them all. I had no interest in human contact.

All I wanted was to be with Eleanor.

So, I spent Christmas Eve surrounded by photo albums and memories. Some were as recent as a few years ago. Others stretched back to our earliest times together. I found some of her old journals, and read her words with indescribable affection.

I spent hours reliving the past. Until the present came crashing back.

Eleanor was dead. Gone forever. I was spending the first Christmas without her in over half a century. The sadness of it was overwhelming.

So, I did something new; I *willingly* became the Beast.

My weak, human body fell prone, and my spiritual form became a monster. Like a ghost 1flew from the empty house, into the sky, and across town. I moved with a purpose, for I knew exactly where I was headed.

Hazel Ridge Cemetery.

There it was. Her grave. A single piece of stone left to remember the woman who touched my life in indescribable ways.

Eleanor Amon
~
1939 — 2009

Tell me something—can you imagine the Beast shedding tears? Until that point, I would have thought the idea laughable.

But here, over her grave, that's exactly what happened.

Deep, mournful howls filled the night. There was more emotion in this sound than any human was capable of. Each syllable radiated misery, communicated on a more instinctive level than words ever could.

The Beast sat there, beating its ethereal claws into the ground. It would have continued for hours, had it not been for the flash of headlights.

A vehicle had come. Interrupted this private moment.

The Beast stood on its hind legs, and glared at the driver. Such an intrusion was unacceptable. I remember thinking the Beast would strike then, claiming its first human victim.

Instead it let out one last, sorrowful howl, and vanished into the wind.

Chapter 8

Time passed, although I don't know what filled it. I must have eaten, and slept, but it was all unconscious. I spent time as the Beast, I remember that much. But honestly, I'm not even sure how many weeks went by like this.

Finally, I had one last, crazy idea.

If it worked, it would all be worth it.

If it failed... I had nothing left to lose.

So why not?

"'Tis night! 'Tis night! And the Devil's light

"Casts glimmering beams around

"The maras dance, the nisses prance

"On the flower-enameled ground"

I spoke the incantation for the second time. At the ritual's close, I sealed my fate with the last step—slicing my arm, mixing blood with water in the basin below.

Every sound in the house silenced. I couldn't even hear my own heartbeat. Complete, utter quiet.

He was here.

I knew it at once. Not just as a voice, whispering in my mind. Moyset was here in the flesh, as much so as He be can at least.

"Hello again, doctor."

The words were from behind me. I turned.

"Isn't this interesting."

His voice was moving. Circling me. I tried to maintain composure, but I was trembling inside.

"Come to ask more miracles thy shant repay? To dig thy tome deeper still?"

If only I could get a look at Him, or at least decide where His voice was coming from. Talking face-to-face, even to a monster, seemed preferable to this. I could sense Him, though. It was strange; it felt like the space he occupied was a void. Moyset's presence was a black hole, the very opposite of existence.

"I... I ask of you a miracle, yes. One that might be beyond your ability," I said.

And then I heard it; a nauseating slithering sound. I couldn't possibly explain it. It was like the coils of some grotesque alien serpent wrapped around the room. The sound of these tendrils moving made me queasy.

"Thy questions my power?"

Moyset was challenged. Good. Maybe He would accept the challenge, and agree to something He otherwise wouldn't. He was right; so far I had a history of bad debt.

"I want to see Eleanor again," I told him. "To hold her in my arms one last time."

The serpentine voice whispered.

"You had thy chance."

"Please, give me another," I said. "I'm useless without her. Just give me the chance to—"

"SILENCE, MORTAL!"

The house shook at the demon's words. I staggered to keep my balance.

"Thou hast already groveled before me, and prayed for my blessing. I hath answered your call, with haste and diligence. Your every wish hath been granted.

"Was thy bride not ill? Was it not terminal? Did I not do the impossible to cure her?"

But... She's gone," I sighed.

"That is by your doing, not mine. You said you desired that spark be in her eyes, and there it sparked. You asked to be with her, and with her you were. Did you expect miracles for nothing? I asked minimal of thee. You had thy wife during the day.

"All you had to do, was give thy nights to me."

"It wasn't like that," I said. My words felt so weak

compared to His. "You tricked me! I thought—"

"*No, thou tricketh me! You desecrated our bargain with doubt and disloyalty. Thou should be grateful I showed mercy.*"

"Mercy? When have you shown me mercy?" I said.

There was that otherworldly slithering again. I got the impression the demon was hissing at me, showing its anger. The room seemed to get smaller the longer we spoke. Was this Thing constrictingthe house? It sure felt like it.

"*Those I cannot trust, I kill. You spoke ill of me, desperate to cheat out of thy deal. I gave thou a second chance. A chance to redeem thyself. A test of loyalty. And once again, mortal, you—failed—ME!*"

I felt lightheaded. Was I running out of oxygen? The air felt thick, like at the top of a tall mountain. He was right of course, about all of it.

"Why, Moyset? Why do you torment me? Do you get your pleasure from watching me suffer?" I said.

Sick laughter cracked through the room. My skull shook with its wretched inflections.

"*Oh doctor, does thou truly believe this is all about thee?*"

I was caught off guard. "What do you mean?"

"*Silly mortal. You, your bride... It's all irrelevant. It never mattered what thy motive was; the only importance was my foothold in this land. We hath waited a long time for just such a fool as yourself.*"

"We?" I said. The implications shocked me. "What do you mean? Who—"

Then it came to me. I knew *exactly* who Moyset was in league with.

"DuPuis."

"*Precisely.*"

"But—why?" I couldn't believe it. "Why would he do this? What could he possibly gain? Tell me, why!"

"*This is the first strike in a shadow war. A war that has been building, in secret, for decades. A war in which I am but a mere soldier. It neither begins with me... Nor ends.*"

What Would Eleanor Do?

Panic raced through me. Suddenly, this was much more than just my problem. It was bigger than me, or Eleanor, or even Elkhorn. If this destroyer, this Dark Horseman, was nothing more than a shock trooper... What could be next?

Standing there, surrounded by fear, I asked myself a question I should have asked months ago.

What would Eleanor do?

It was amazing. Throughout this entire nightmare, never once did I ask such a simple question. If Eleanor were here, in her right mind, what would she tell me to do?

Of course, the answer came immediately.

Eleanor never would have made such an arrangement. Would never have let me sell my soul for her. She was much too brave for that. She would rather go down fighting than resort to such measure.

Well, I guess it's too late for that.

But what would she do *now?* Standing up to a demon, who threatened the safety of all she knew. I knew what she would *not* do—she would never let anyone push her around. Eleanor Amon would not be bullied or walked on. So why should I be? If I went down fighting, then perhaps I would see her in the afterlife.

Wait... That's it.

I knew what I had to do.

"You were right, Moyset," I said. "I have no right asking you for anything more. I have not done my part."

There was a satisfactory cooing noise. It was somehow more sickening than the sounds of anger.

"But you never should have taken Eleanor from me. That was your biggest mistake."

"Is that so? What makes you think so, hm?"

"Because now you have no leverage over me," I said.

Slowly yet confidently, I lifted the ritual knife to eye

Chapter 8

level. The blade still glistened with my blood from the summoning.

Moyset sounded upset.

"What are you doing?"

"Ending this," I said.

I focused my mind completely on Eleanor. I still don't know if there is an afterlife... Or an ending. All I know is I wanted my last thoughts to be of her.

My eyes were closed.

My thoughts on Eleanor.

My hand raised.

And, in one final moment of bravery, I swung the blade toward my heart.

Chapter 9:
The Horseman's New Mount

The blade nicked my skin. That was all.

It stopped, and try as I might I couldn't force it down any further. Something held it back.

"Wrong again, doctor. Tonight is no ending."

My hand withdrew, against my will.

"At least... Not for me."

With all my strength, I made one final effort to pierce my heart. I pushed and pushed. My hand rocked back and forth, struggling against an invisible foe.

If I was going to die, I was taking this demon with me.

"You were right about one thing, however. Your usefulness... Has run out."

From the shadows came another horrid sound, part hiss and part grunt. The knife was knocked out of my hand and across the room.

I dove for it, but something hit me hard from behind. I collapsed, the wind blown from my chest. Before I could

Chapter 9

catch my breath, those unseen tendrils tightened around my neck.

Panicked, I grabbed at my neck, but couldn't touch the bindings. Moyset was strangling me with a ghostly hand, and I couldn't do a thing about it.

"But mayhap there is a way to grant your last request."

Choking. Struggling for breath.

"Yes... That can be arranged. Not for free, of course. The cost is heavy, and this time thou shalt not escape it."

Getting lightheaded. Everything's blurry. The demon's voice got softer, whispering into my ear.

"Thou must pay with the blood of the innocent. And then..."

I glanced up. In my asphyxiation, I thought I saw eyes staring down at me.

"You may rejoin your beloved Eleanor."

Dark cackling rang in my ears. My last thought was fear—not just for myself, but everyone that I loved.

Then the Dark Horseman rode my soul into the wind.

This transformation was unlike before. Normally, I had some measure of control, or at least influence, over the Beast. This time, He was the only one in command.

Hatred pulsed through my ethereal body like blood. Everything I saw was through a fiery haze. The air itself rippled with heat. I didn't know where I was going, but I felt there was a deadly purpose to the Beast.

Then it descended upon its target.

I remember him as red—that's how I saw him, anyway. No features or anything distinguishable. Just red.

The Beast pounced.

Whoever this red target was, he didn't stand a chance. The Beast now was stronger than ever. Not a weak shade like when it first arrived in Elkhorn. Now, the Beast was a true monster, capable of terrible damage.

The Horseman's New Mount

I felt claws cut through skin. Teeth sink into flesh. I tasted blood in my mouth. It wasn't until I heard the screams that I recognized the poor victim.

It was Barbason.

Then red turned to black, and I faded from consciousness.

I awoke to the noonday sun.

Something was different. I could feel it immediately, although I couldn't tell what it was. Was I hungry? No, that wasn't it. Groggy? Not quite that, either. After a moment of analysis, I realized what was wrong.

I was lighter.

Some burden had been lifted off my shoulders, and I walked free again. For the first time since returning from France, my mind was quiet. No voices, no horrible whispers. My mind was my own. I was free.

Relief didn't last.

What happened to Barbason? I knew it was him. And to suddenly wake up and be rid of Moyset?

It was too good to be true. Something had to be wrong.

I had to find my brother. Had to make sure he was safe, and warn him about Dr. DuPuis. Together, maybe, we could stop this "shadow war," or at least put up some kind of resistance.

Maybe, just maybe, it wasn't too late.

I sped down the road to B.R. Amon & Sons, Inc.

Bang, bang, bang, I pounded at the door. I prayed that, if there was a God, he hadn't lost faith in me. Prayed that my brother would answer. That he was alright. I pictured him

Chapter 9

lying there, his body shattered from the Beast's mauling. How could he survive that?

I already killed my wife. Had I just killed my brother as well?

Thankfully, Barbason answered the door.

"Connor?" he said. "What are ye doin' here?"

I grabbed my brother into a hug. I was panicked, and before I could think I blurted out, "I never should have called him! Never should have made another deal!"

Barbason froze. I let go, and got a good look at him. That's when I first noticed that something was different. It was his eyes, mostly. They had always been simple, yet warm. Reclusive but well-meaning.

Not anymore.

There was darkness in his eyes. A black fire burning beneath the surface. I shivered. At some instinctive level, I knew to fear him now.

"Brother," he said. "Ye tell me once, and ye tell me straight. What did ye do?"

Where to begin? I had to tell him everything, somehow, so that we could work together to stop it. If only I could skip to the end, ignore the part where my own weakness opened Pandora's Box again.

But I couldn't. It was time to face the music.

"Barbason, I... Made another mistake. I summoned Moyset again. This time, I asked the unthinkable—I wanted Him to bring Eleanor back from the grave." The more I spoke, the worse I felt. I couldn't restrain the tears. There, on his doorstep, I choked out the words. "Moyset could do it, at the price of an innocent life..."

Then it all became real. I knew what Moyset had done. I *knew* he had taken my brother, much like he took me. I don't know how, but I knew it was true.

Barbason paid the price for my folly.

The Horseman's New Mount

Everything crashed down on me. I broke into delirious sobs. Had I really condemned my brother to this tortured existence? Oh God, what have I done?

"I didn't know it was you! I never thought it was you!" I cried into my hands.

When I looked up, my spine turned to ice.

My brother looked down at me with blazing anger. His nostrils flared, and his lips curled into a snarl. I could see veins throbbing in his neck.

"Last night. That was ye," he muttered. "Ye came an' attacked me, didn't ye?"

My throat went dry. Words escaped me under that stare.

"Ye could've killed me! Ye nearly *did* kill me!"

"I—I'm so sorry," I said. I had to get a grip. There was too much left to explain. "Listen, there's more. Moyset, he told me that—"

"Out," he interrupted.

I stood up, my jaw hanging open. "Brother... Brother, I—"

Barbason grabbed me by the collar, and jerked me closer. I felt feverish heat radiate off of him.

"Ye'll pay for this, Connor," he growled. "Ye should've learned when ye had the chance. Mark my words, ye'll pay..."

When he threw me, I went halfway across the lot.

I landed hard against the cement. The wind escaped my lungs again. All I could do was gasp for air, and look back at the doorway.

What I saw was terrible.

Barbason stood there, a silhouette against the light from the house. His eyes glared down at me, the lines of his face etched into primal rage. Behind him, I swear I saw something else. A great shadow, looming above and behind

Chapter 9

him. A shadow which pulled all the strings. A shadow that lurked over me just a day earlier.

Moyset, the Dark Horseman, rode a new mount now.

Epilogue:

Love

And that's it; the whole story. Everything that's happened to this point, for better or worse.

I find myself back in the living room, pacing restlessly in front of the kindling fire. Soon, I fear, Barbason will come. If he does, he will probably kill me, and I'll be reunited with Eleanor once again.

Looks like Moyset might keep his word, after all.

But I cannot give up. Not yet.

Barbason needs to know the *whole* truth. He threw me out before I could explain what the demon said, about this "shadow war" and Dr. DuPuis' true allegiance.

It might not be too late. We still have a chance.

Dr. DuPuis is the enemy. I don't know if he is ultimately behind all of this, or if he answers to someone (or some*thing!*) greater still. He took advantage of my weakness before, but this time...

This time, I won't be alone.

Together, perhaps Barbason and I could get the truth

Epilogue

out of DuPuis. It's a long shot, I know—but it's the only shot we have.

If I have to plead with my brother to listen, I'll do it. He has such a gentle heart. Even under the influence of Moyset, I believe Barbason will hear me out before passing judgment.

At least, I hope so.

If not... Well, then I will die trying.

I should apologize. My story has not been a happy one. Perhaps much of that is my fault. I brought this demon to Elkhorn. I brought this curse upon those I love. I should have turned back the second I saw DuPuis' diabolical grin, but I didn't. I made one terrible choice after another.

It sounds mad. Perhaps it is. But please, remember this one, important thing...

I'm not insane.

I'm in love.

And if this all happened to you... Would you have the strength to say no?

Thanks for reading
Tale of the Gévaudan Beast!

~

If you enjoyed it, would you mind taking a few minutes of your time to leave a review on Amazon? It doesn't take long, and it makes all the difference. I know I look at reviews before picking up a book, and I'm sure future readers will appreciate hearing what you have to say.

And don't worry—this is truly just the beginning. There's a lot to come in the *Enoc Tales*, and I can't wait to share it with you.

If you want to keep up on all the news and cool stuff related to the series, why not subscribe to my newsletter? The sign-up form is on the official website, **www.EnocTales.com**.

Again, thanks for joining me in this adventure. Looking forward to our next one together!

Don't stop now!
Turn the page to find out what happens next. Included is the Prologue & First Chapter of **Tale of the Wisconsin Werewolf**, with never-before-seen extra scenes.

Edison T. Crux

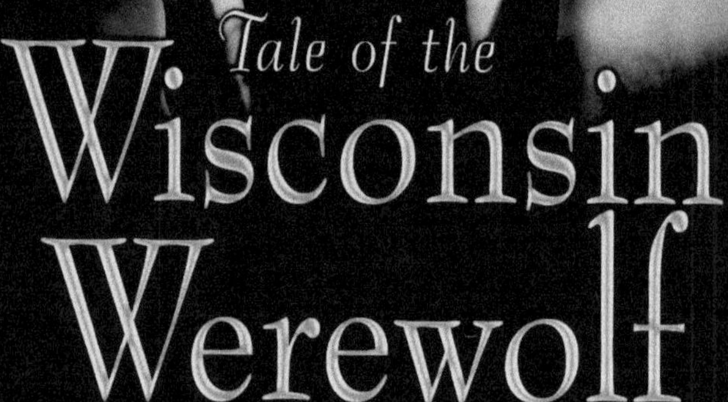

Tale of the
Wisconsin
Werewolf

The Enoc Tales Book 1

Prologue:
Retribution

Retribution.

That is the reason for my existence. Retribution.

A trail of despicable choices brought it to this. With every decision, a justification; the wrong choice looked right and the right choice looked too hard. He dug this hole. Now the weight of a thousand selfish deeds pile up, one by one, until he is buried in them. His actions forged his tomb.

Retribution.

He must pay for his sins. Intention does not excuse action.

Under the cover of the starless night I find him, pacing sleeplessly in his home. Is he troubled by what he has done, or worried that he could be held accountable?

Retribution.

I look through the window. The room is illuminated by nothing but the gentle glow of the hearth. He does not see me. Not yet.

With a mighty leap I shatter the window. He turns to see his punisher standing in the wreckage of broken glass. The man is afraid, yes... But not surprised. He knew this night was coming.

Prologue

Retribution.

We stare at each other. Orange light from the fire ebbs and flows over his face, pulsing like the beat of a heart.

"I... I never meant for it to come to this," he says. If he only knew the irony of these words. From his mouth they are hollow and meaningless.

I growl, and he steps back. Coward. He knows better than anyone that there is no escaping his fate.

"P—please!" he whimpers. "Don't kill me!"

The fire blazes brighter and faster, keeping pace with the fool's heart. I bare my teeth in a snarl and he runs. Runs! Like he has a life worth sparing. Like he doesn't deserve what's coming.

He retreats no more than a step when I pounce, a predator claiming its prey. Deep cuts turn his back to bloody canyons.

Retribution.

The man falls. He attempts to crawl away, but I won't allow it. My powerful claw sinks into his side and flips him over briskly.

I want him to see me as he dies.

He yelps as his fresh wounds hit the floor. His eyes reveal a pitiable array of emotions; hopelessness, desperation, terror. Not a trace of willingness to pay the price of his deeds.

"D—don't do this to me!" he cries. "It might not be too late. We might still be able to—"

A sharp growl interrupts him. I press my horrific face to his. The livid fury in my eyes send a clear message. Look at me, *these eyes say.* Look at me and tell me it's not too late!

Tears drenched the fool's cheeks. "Please..." He mutters one last time.

I grab him by the collar, and hurl him into the fireplace.

I watch as the flames consume him. Embers flicker out from the hearth and catch the carpet. Before long, the room is blanketed with a hungry fire.

His last moments alive were a living Hell.

Retribution.

Retribution

Slowly, the old man got up.

Although his body was back, everything was still in a fiery red haze. That one word still pulsed to the beat of his heart.

Retribution.

He remembered what just happened as if it were a vivid dream. Vivid, but abstract. Like all of the human thoughts were disconnected, and left his waking mind to translate the feelings of something far more primal.

Then he heard the voice.

"Welcome."

Startled, the old man looked around. "Who's there?"

The room was dark, filled with shadows that could hide untold dangers. Which one held this monster?

"I am the end of all you were, and I am the beginning of all we shall be."

Suddenly, he knew with grave certainty the owner of this voice. And he knew exactly what this meant for him.

"It's true…" he said. "It's all true. Now, I'm…"

"Yes… Now, you are mine."

Then there was nothing he could do. The old man dropped down, his heart aching.

The man at fault was dead, but he wasn't the one to pay the final price.

Retribution, indeed.

Chapter 1:
Funerals

This was a winter of funerals.

Last time the ground was clear of snow, fifteen year-old Will Lewis was happy to say he had never been to a funeral. That might not be something to brag about, but rather to give thanks in the silence of your own mind. In fact, Will's childhood was free from any tragedy worse than a bad flu season.

That is, until recently.

For the second time this season Will stood with his parents at Hazel Ridge Cemetery. You needed no directions to find the grave-side service; dozens and dozens of mourners in black coats stood out against the white snow and gray headstones. There were almost as many living as there were dead in this quiet Wisconsin graveyard.

As family of the deceased, Will and his parents were flooded with condolences. Despite the cold air Will felt hot and uncomfortable, and not just because of his suit. It was awkward to greet an endless stream of teary-eyed people he

Funerals

barely knew, if at all. One man Will hadn't met until that moment gave him a tight, sobbing hug.

I should be used to it by now, he thought. *We went through this a few months ago.*

But last time was different, wasn't it? Grandma Eleanor had *Creutzfeldt–Jakob* Disease, a fatal condition that slowly stole her personality and memories. Sure, she started getting better, but when a heart attack claimed her life the people of Elkhorn already pictured a world without sweet old Eleanor Amon.

A heavyset woman in a black wool coat joined them. Will was grateful to see a familiar face. Her name was Julie Baker. Although Julie and Will's mother were best friends growing up, they rarely saw each other after Cassandra Amon moved to Beloit to become Mrs. Lewis. But old friends become close in a hurry when surrounded by strangers.

Mrs. Baker and Will's mom met eyes. Silence was enough of a greeting for them.

"How are you holding up, Cassy?" Mrs. Baker asked.

"I'm here," she said quietly, and left it at that.

Will expected his mother to be in tears. Certainly more than a few were shed at her mother's funeral in December. But today, Cassandra Lewis (previously Amon) stood with her head held high and her eyes determinedly dry. Will swelled with pride at that fact.

After all, they were about to bury her father.

It was no great shock to Will that his grandfather, Connor Amon, passed away less than two months after Grandma Eleanor. Wives usually live longer. Husbands, it seems, often follow closely behind their dearly beloved. It's almost as if they lose more than a spouse; that some vital part of their being is torn away, a wound that will eventually bleed the life out of them.

Connor felt responsible for his wife's death. One look

Chapter 1

in the grieving man's eyes was all it took to see that. He hadn't been the same since Eleanor was diagnosed with CJD. You see, Connor Amon wasn't just a neurologist; he literally wrote the *book* on neurology. Textbooks with his name on the cover were required reading at medical colleges nationwide. But even the great Dr. Amon couldn't cure his wife.

No, it didn't surprise Will that Grandpa Connor had died. What surprised him was *how* he died.

Another group of bereaved strangers offered condolences. Will sensed his mother's well-contained tears on the verge of breaking. He wasn't the only one who sensed it; Will's father took the initiative of shepherding the new arrivals towards the memorial display. The mourners fussed, but John Lewis left no room for argument. He was stern. Held to his word. And loved his wife and child deeply, even if he rarely showed it.

The interruption averted, Will's mind returned to Grandpa Connor's unusual death.

This is what Will was told: Late last Wednesday (which always sounds better as "the night of February the 10th"), one of Connor's neighbors reported smoke coming from the doctor's house. By the time the fire department arrived, it was too late for poor Grandpa Connor. They said the fire was an accident.

It wasn't a bad story. The only problem is it wasn't true.

Will spent the following nights with his ear to his door, listening to his parents (some might call it *eavesdropping*, but Will preferred to think of it as mere curiosity). He couldn't hear them clearly, but from the words he could make out *("arson," "broken in," "intruder")*, Will pieced together a theory.

Connor Amon was murdered.

Everyone was beckoned to the coffin, filling up the

Funerals

seats under the canopy. The clergy was about to begin the grave-side funeral service. As the clergy made his eulogy and read a few verses from the Bible, Will puzzled over his theory. There was one important element that didn't make sense; who would want Dr. Amon dead?

He was a doctor, not a lawyer or business executive. He was never accused of medical malpractice, in fact he had an outstanding track record. Surely no one could murder him based on his profession.

Connor was charitable. He didn't live luxuriously, and donated more money to the library, schools and hospital than most people made in a year.

Will's mother was the primary beneficiary of Connor's estate. She had the most to gain financially, but was miles from Elkhorn at the time of her father's demise.

Who, then, would murder Connor? As far as Will could figure, no one else had anything to gain. Except, perhaps...

Will looked through the crowd, but couldn't find him. At last, when he craned his neck around he spotted the person he was looking for.

Barbason Amon.

Separated from the mourners, the old man was leaning against a mausoleum watching the funeral service with mild attention. His long, thinning hair was a mess of tangles and split ends. That face could have been carved of wood; sharp features, deep eye sockets, a rough stubble, and a flat, emotionless face. Barbason was Connor's younger brother, although few would have guessed it. Connor's enthusiasm kept him youthful, while Barbason aged faster than his time.

Could Uncle Barbason have killed his own brother?

Doubtful, Will concluded. His great-uncle was antisocial, but he never seemed dangerous. Just an old man

Chapter 1

who minded his own business, and would thank you to do the same. He did remember the brothers talking in hushed voices at Grandma Eleanor's funeral, however. That was unusual, but hardly reason to worry.

As the eulogy finished, Will began to think his imagination got the better of him. Maybe Grandpa Connor hadn't been murdered. Maybe it really *was* just an accident.

… Or maybe there was more to it than Will knew.

After the service, people lingered. No one seemed ready to leave Connor's side, so they stayed and talked to each other, despite the brisk chill nipping at their skin. Will didn't expect his family to stick around; mourning alongside strangers might be comforting to some, but not to the Lewis'.

Will's father pulled him aside.

"Son," he said. "Your mother and I need to speak to your uncle. Would you be alright for a few minutes on your own?"

Will knew that tone. It was a *don't argue with me* tone. The way he said it wasn't mean, but it *was* adamant. Will nodded, and his parents left a trail in the snow leading to the mausoleum Barbason had claimed. The old man sized them up as they approached.

Not wanting to intrude, Will took a stroll down the cemetery path. His eyes idly read the names on headstones while his mind continued to question the newest resident of Hazel Ridge.

In his lack of attention, Will walked right into somebody. They both staggered to keep their feet on the ground

"Oh, I'm sorry," Will said. His arms flailed as he tried to keep his balance.

"It's fine," said a girl's voice.

Funerals

When Will looked up, he almost *did* lose lose his footing. The girl he bumped into had to be around his age, give or take a year. It took a single glance for Will's heart to speed up a notch. The girl's red hair was silky and smooth, flowing from her winter hat to below her shoulders. She had a kind of carefree youthfulness that shined through her face. When she met his gaze, Will blushed; those eyes were such a brilliant shade of green they almost sparkled.

She was the prettiest girl Will ever met.

He forced his eyes away. Will was embarrassed enough for bumping into her, he didn't need to make it worse by staring. But when silence followed the girl started to walk away.

"Are you here for the funeral?" Will blurted out. It sounded stupid, but he had to say *something;* he didn't want her to leave yet.

She turned towards Will. "Yeah. My dad knew him, and wanted to pay his respects." She smiled. "He dragged me along."

Will laughed. It came out at a higher pitch than he hoped.

"How did you know Dr. Amon?" the girl asked.

In the distance, Will noticed his parents talking to Barbason. It didn't look friendly. "He was my grandpa," said Will.

"Oh wow, I'm sorry," she said. The girl examined him more closely. "Do you live around here? I don't recognize you."

Will suddenly wished he was from the area. Suddenly Elkhorn was much more appealing. "I live in Beloit, actually. It's about a half hour drive." It was a struggle to sound casual; Will thought his heart had taken on life of its own, beating at such a frantic pace. He couldn't remember when he last had feeling in his legs.

Chapter 1

This girl, on the other hand, seemed perfectly at ease. "Ah, that explains it. I've got connections around here, but you're outside of my reach!" She smiled and held out a gloved hand. "My name's Eliza."

Will felt queasy as they shook hands. Captivated by her smile, he momentarily forgot how to speak. The memory returned with a crash, and finally he understood he had to introduce *himself* too. "I'm Will," he said at last. "Will Lewis."

"Well, nice to meet you, Will," said Eliza. "I should probably find my dad before he thinks I'm avoiding the funeral."

"Yeah, I need to get back to my parents too." Will tried not to sound disappointed. He was in no hurry to see her go.

Eliza winked. "Who knows, maybe we'll see each other next time you're in town."

With Grandpa Connor gone, Will didn't see any occasion to return to Elkhorn. He made a mental note to think of excuses to come back, just for the chance to cross paths again. Eliza waved and headed off towards the canopy, where the number of people finally started to diminish.

For the first time all day, Will's mind wasn't on his grandfather's death. In fact, he was quite proud of himself; he talked to a pretty girl, and didn't make a *complete* fool of himself (well, aside from blindly running into her and nearly knocking them both over). He would probably never see her again, but his mood had certainly improved.

Within minutes, that would change again.

Will strolled down the paths, using his memory like a video; it rewound to meeting Eliza, paused at every smile, then replayed the scene over and over. His knees still felt a little shaky, but at least his pulse stopped its crazy tap-dance.

X

Funerals

Just as Will pictured that last, playful wink, there was a commotion by the canopy.

Will rushed back. The sight coming into view shocked him; it was his father, fist clenched around Barbason's collar, pinning the old man to the mausoleum. Only a handful of visitors remained, but they rushed to break up the confrontation. Will's mother buried her face in her hands, the tears flowing at last.

"What the devil is going on here?" said the clergy. "This is a *funeral!*"

Mr. Lewis and Barbason were motionless, their eyes locked with laser focus.

"Would you kindly put that man down?" the clergy pleaded.

Slowly, Barbason slid down the stone wall. Even as Mr. Lewis released his grip he didn't break his gaze.

Through her tears, Mrs. Lewis managed to smile at her son. "C'mon hun, I think it's time to go," she said, leading Will back to the car. Mr. Lewis finally turned from Barbason to follow his wife.

"Yer father ain't no saint, Cass!" Barbason yelled after them. His voice was gruff, like an old dog's bark.

The words sent a chill down Will's spine. His mother cried. His father walked briskly, jaw clenched.

Will glanced over his shoulder. Barbason's eyes followed them with unnerving intensity. When he was safely in the car, Will realized he was holding his breath. He let out a sigh of relief, and was glad to leave the gates of Hazel Ridge Cemetery.

The building shook when Barbason slammed the door.

("Connor was a good man, Barbason. You hear me? A good

Chapter 1

man!")

("My father's acting strange for months...")

("There's more to his death, and you know it. I saw the way you two have been talking. You're hiding something, Barbason. And I'll find out what it is.")

The conversation repeated endlessly in his mind. Barbason reached the kitchen and slammed a fist into the counter.

"Fools, the lot o' them," he mumbled. "*'Conner was a good man,'* my ass! He deserved death. Deserved it long before he got it!"

The room sweltered like a furnace. Barbason's anger was a fire, hot enough to burn.

Hot enough to *kill.*

He splashed water from the faucet over his face. It soothed him, but only mildly. He needed a distraction. Something to take his mind away from his niece and her pigheaded husband.

Holding his walking stick in a vice grip, Barbason went to the garage. Now that the business was shut down, he only came here for one thing.

To carve.

Against one wall were blocks of wood, cut from larger planks. Barbason grabbed one, sat down, and took out his best carving knife. There was a time when he thought of what to sculpt, and carefully followed his mind's eye to bring it to life.

But now they all came out the same.

Barbason violently chipped pieces of wood from the block, with no apparent reason or plan. Wood shavings showered the garage floor. Not once did he pay attention to what he was making.

Finally, Barbason found himself holding a statue of a man with the head of a wolf.

Funerals

Seeing it did nothing to calm him. He slammed it on the table, along with a collection of similar carvings. Hoping to ride his rage out this way, Barbason grabbed the next wood block. He tore it apart, shred by shred, until there was nothing left but a wooden wolf's paw. He threw it against the wall and vented his anger on the next piece, a blank cube that would soon be a monstrous jawbone.

("There's more to his death, and you know it")

"Damn right I know it," Barbason grunted. He could hardly see through the searing heat. "I know all 'bout it! After all, I was the one who killed 'em!"

The half-finished sculpture hit the floor. Barbason did everything he could to control himself... But he knew what was coming.

The Change started. Each enraged beat of his heart pumped hatred into his veins, and each breath exhaled a piece of his humanity.

As Barbason lost himself, a single word crept up his spine.

Retribution.

The Lewis family stopped for dinner at the Elk Creek Bar & Grill. During her youth, Will's mother came here every Friday night for the fish fry. Although it was Sunday and no fish were frying, "The Elk" was a fitting place to honor her father.

It was a quiet dinner. No one said more than an occasional comment on their food (Will's parents both order "Elk Burgers," a local tradition. Being a self-proclaimed vegetarian, Will was happy with grilled cheese and french fries).

Will needed all of his self-control not to ask what the argument was about. Not knowing drove him crazy with

Chapter 1

curiosity, but Mr. Lewis was gripping his burger tight enough to break the bun. Not a sign of calming down. So Will held his tongue, at least for a bit longer.

Once they were well fed, the Lewis' got back in their car for the trip back to Beloit. It was already dark, and the snow that came in gentle flakes earlier now fell in flurries. Mr. Lewis let the car warm up before driving, and Will sensed an opportunity.

"That was quite a funeral," he said.

Mr. Lewis didn't respond. Mrs. Lewis nodded and said "I think Grandpa Connor would have been happy to see how many people came."

"Yeah." Will tried to pick his words carefully. "It seems like everyone really liked him."

Mrs. Lewis gave a pained smiled. "He did a lot of good, for a lot of people."

The car pulled out of the parking lot. There weren't many cars on the roads in town, but those that were out were driving slowly tonight. The wind was picking up, bombarding the windshield with snowflakes.

"Did Uncle Barbason like him?" Will asked.

This time, silence was his only response.

"I mean, I don't remember seeing them together a lot," Will continued. "Except at Grandma Eleanor's funeral. I saw them talking a lot then."

As they merged onto highway I-43, the car felt colder than it did without the heater. "They... Had very different interests," Mrs. Lewis finally said.

"What were they talking about? Do you know?"

Mr. Lewis spoke for the first time since dinner. "You would have to ask your great-uncle."

"Was that what you asked him?" Will said. Once the floodgate of questions was open, he couldn't stop himself.

"That's not important," Mr. Lewis said.

Funerals

"He sounded angry."

"He might have been."

"What were you talking about?"

"Nothing."

"Was it about Grandma Eleanor?"

"No."

"Grandpa Connor?"

"Leave it alone, son."

"Was it about Mom?"

"That's *enough*, William," Mr. Lewis said loudly.

Will shrunk into his seat. He found his boundary, and pushed it one question too far. He had a feeling it was going to be a very quiet car ride.

They drove through the snow without another word. Will watched the open countryside; even though it was night time, the sheet of snow reflected enough light to see the passing landscape.

Something caught his attention. In the distance, a dark spot stood out against the backdrop of white. It was too far to make out any shape, only the indistinct silhouette of an object not covered in snow. Will thought it was odd, and wondered with only half-interest what it could be.

Then the silhouette moved.

In that moment goosebumps covered Will's body. He didn't expect it to be *alive*. There was no mistaking its movements; the mystery spot was some kind of animal. And, judging from the speed and direction, it was an animal with a purpose.

Will had a grim realization as he traced its path. *It's headed towards the highway!*

"D-Dad," he said, his voice quivering. "What's that?"

Mr. Lewis glanced over for just a moment. In this weather, he needed to keep his eyes on the road. "Probably just a cow, son."

Chapter 1

As the shadow got closer, Will saw two tiny yellow lights on the creature. *Eyes,* he thought. *Its eyes are reflecting light from the cars.* Will had the horrible impression the eyes were looking right at him.

"Seriously Dad, what *is* that?" he said. He was quickly rising to panic.

What came next happened so fast, Will could barely keep up.

Within seconds the silhouette was nearly to the road, on a collision course with their car. Will had just enough time to wonder if the creature was aware of the speeding vehicle before the shape (huge from this distance) leapt high off the ground. A moment of silence. Then, with a thunderous boom, the car shook violently off its lane. The metal roof sunk in from the weight of impact.

That thing landed on us!

Mr. Lewis swore. He tried to regain control of the car, but the back wheels fishtailed in the fresh snow.

Before Will could grasp one thing that happened, another interrupted him.

Will started to say "What's going on?" But his voice caught in his throat as he saw it; the dark shape of a gigantic claw swinging in front of the windshield. The sound of shattering glass was nothing compared to the relentless howling of the wind, hitting them headfirst at over 65 miles per hour. Will covered his face before being showered in glass shards.

He couldn't see, but he could feel. He felt pain as dozens of cuts lacerated his body. He felt freezing wind choke the breath from his lungs. He felt the car sway dangerously.

Will peered out from the cover of his arms for just a second. His eyes instantly dried up and stung, but he caught a glimpse of what was happening.

Funerals

That claw reached forward, pinning Mr. Lewis to his seat. He wasn't moving.

Mrs. Lewis was struggling to free her husband. She was drenched in blood, large pieces of glass still caught in her skin.

And, barely visible against the dark background, was the face of the creature.

Will couldn't see its shape or features. But he saw those eyes; two glowing yellow embers taken from the hearth of Hell.

The car shook again.

The wheels turned, out of control.

They left pavement.

Spun wildly.

And then, with a final ear-splitting crash, Will was unconscious.

In the land of dreams, nightmares are king. You might go years without having one, but when they do show up they demand your attention like no other dream can.

Time means nothing in nightmares. For that reason, Will had no idea how long he was sleeping. But whether he was out for an hour or a week, he spent every second of it locked in perpetual memory of the car crash.

Many details evolved with each replaying, becoming something they never truly were. The landscape changed to a much grander setting than I-43. Snow flurries became an all-out blizzard. And despite the wind stinging his eyes Will started to see the entire event unfold, as if watching it on TV while safely curled up at home.

Each time, the creature became more terrifying.

Even in his dreams, Will never got a good look at it. Fear of the unknown is highly distilled. It leaves your

Chapter 1

imagination to come up with one horrific possibility after another. The only thing Will could clearly see were the eyes. They haunted every moment of his dreams.

Those eyes lingered in Will's mind when, finally, he woke up.

Consciousness was a relief. It meant Will could finally escape the endless loop of nightmares. Gradually, he took in his surroundings. He was in a hospital, which didn't surprise him at all. A nurse was next to him, checking his vitals.

"Good morning," said the nurse. "How are you feeling?"

Will squinted, still adjusting to the light. "Sore," he said. His body was covered in dull aches, and his head was pounding. Will had the feeling it would be much worse, if it weren't for the modern miracle of pain medication.

She consulted her chart. "I bet you are. Looks like you're recovering well though."

Will massaged his forehead, to find a large bandage covering it. Several smaller wrappings were scattered across his arms. Suddenly, a question rushed to him. "Are my parents okay?"

The nurse stiffened, but her voice remained even. "Just try and rest for now. Dr. Thompson will be in later."

Not leaving much time for argument, the nurse left. Will fell back asleep with an uneasiness in the pit of his stomach.

By the time the doctor came, Will was awake again. Dr. Thompson was an older man, with comically-bushy eyebrows and mustache. His expression, however, was not so comical.

"Ah, hello Will," he said in a husky voice. "How are you feeling?"

That always seemed like a silly question to ask someone lying in a hospital bed. "Alright, I guess."

Funerals

The doctor took a seat next to the bed. "I expect you've felt better. You suffered from a mild concussion. Aside from that you have an impressive collection of cuts and bruises, none of which severe."

Will tried to move, but a fresh wave of aches changed his mind. He hoped it was almost time for more medication, because he was beginning to feel like one giant bruise.

"Have you felt any dizziness, nausea, or lack of motor skills?" the doctor asked.

Will shook his head.

"Any sensitivity to light, blurred vision, or ringing in your ears?"

"A little bit of the light sensitivity," Will admitted. "But none of the other stuff."

"Good," Dr. Thompson was taking notes as they spoke. "Now Will... Do you remember what happened last night?"

Will's temperature dropped.

He remembered the creature.

He remembered a crash.

And boy, did he ever remember those eyes.

Or did he? His sleep was filled with nightmares, reshaping the event in more horrific detail. Awake now, he wasn't sure how much of it really happened.

"I'm not sure," Will said. "I was having... A lot of dreams. It all sort of blurs together."

Dr. Thompson scribbled another note. "That's fine. Post-traumatic amnesia is common with head injuries of this nature." His expression turned grave as he put down his clipboard. "Will, you were in a very serious accident last night. While on the highway, your car slid across the median into oncoming traffic. You collided head-first with another vehicle, resulting in a four car pile-up."

Perhaps Will spoke too soon about the nausea; his

Chapter 1

stomach suddenly felt ready to empty its contents.

"Are my parents okay?" Will asked.

The doctor let out a heavy sigh. "Paramedics were there as soon as possible... But it was bad. Your father passed away before they arrived. They did everything they could for your mother, but she died on the way to the hospital." He put his hand on Will's arm. "I'm so sorry, Will."

It was like a switch was turned off in Will's mind, shutting off all thought and feeling. He was frozen in his place, unable to comprehend what he just heard. Dr. Thompson kept talking, but the words flowed meaninglessly through the air, the connection from ears to brain lost. He didn't hear the doctor stand up, but the sound of the closing door faintly registered.

Will was alone now.

Alone in the room.

Alone in his life.

He cried. There were no tears. Just deep, hollow sobs. Eventually, he cried himself back to sleep.

It was early morning when Will got the news from Dr. Thompson. The next time he woke up, it was past four o'clock. Mercifully, this sleep was completely dreamless. Will's mind was still too numb to think, and certainly couldn't conjure up something as complex as a dream. The nurse brought him a plate of food, which he ate in auto-pilot.

Subconsciously, Will refused to believe that his parents were gone. Since he had no rational hope to cling to, his solution was to forgo thought entirely.

Shortly after Will's meal, the door opened. He expected to see the nurse, or perhaps Dr. Thompson.

But he certainly *didn't* expect his great-uncle, Barbason.

XX

Funerals

The old man stood in the doorway, hesitant to enter. He finally stepped inside, leaning heavily on his wooden cane.

"Hey kid."

Will had no idea what to say. He could probably count the times he spoke with his great-uncle on one hand. Not to mention, of course, that the last time Will saw him he had nearly gotten into a brawl with his dad. "Hi..."

Barbason sat down. "Ye feelin' alright?"

"Sure," said Will, who felt anything but alright.

"I heard 'bout the accident." Barbason sounded just as uncomfortable as Will felt. "I'm sorry."

"It's okay." Will didn't want to address the issue of his parents. He brushed the topic aside as lightly as he could.

The old man cleared his throat. There was a long, awkward pause before Barbason spoke again. "Listen, they was askin' 'bout ye, and what all ye had as for family. Wanted to know if yer dad had any relatives, stuff like that."

In his denial, Will hadn't thought about where he would live. The more he considered it, the worse it looked. "Dad was an only child. Both of his parents died when I was young."

"Yeah, that's what I was figurin'. I told 'em I didn't think his folks were 'round no more." Barbason fiddled with his cane, keeping his eyes there instead of on Will. "They, er... Well, seeing as we're related and all, they asked if it'd be alright if ye stay with me."

Will tensed up. He didn't like the sound of this. "What did you tell them?"

"Said I'd ask what ye wanted."

"I want my parents," Will said flatly.

Barbason looked directly at Will, his eyes flooded with remorse. You couldn't tell this was the same man who shouted harsh words at his brother's funeral.

XXI

Chapter 1

"I wish I could do that for ye, kid. I really do. But the best I've got is a roof and a bed. It's not much, but if ye want it... It's yours."

Will laid back on his pillow. He couldn't ignore reality any longer; he was now an orphan. Fighting back tears, he considered his options. If he turned down his great-uncle's offer, chances are Will would live in an orphanage. Maybe, if he was lucky, he might get into a foster home.

The truth is, Will didn't like any of his options. But something about the sadness in his great-uncle's eyes made him feel connected to the old man. They might not know each other well, but ultimately they were still family.

"Alright," Will said. "If you'll have me, I'll stay with you."

Order Now!

Pick up your copy at
WisconsinWerewolf.com

Acknowledgements

I'd like to thank everyone who helped make this book what it is. I had a great support team throughout, and a fantastic group of beta-readers who made this story shine.

Big thanks to:

Katie Crux

Mark & Camille Peltier-Robson

Devin Peltier-Robson

Brenda

Jacob Faust

Kathleen Ludwig

Peter Doherty

Hunter Thaw

Lewis "Cylver" Thorpe

Raymond Z.

Chris A. Trigon

Roger Simmons

Connor C.

And thank YOU for reading this book!
Fans like you are what make it all worth it.

Further Research

——

The Beast of Bray Road by Linda Godfrey. Linda is the expert on the REAL Wisconsin Werewolf legend. This is the book that inspired my interest in the topic, and ultimately led me to write these stories.

The Real Wolfman, a video documentary featured on the History Channel. A great show about the most gruesome "werewolf" attack in history. *The Beast of Gévaudan* isn't fiction, and if you want to know more this documentary will get you started.

Actually, an internet search for the *Beast of Gévaudan* will turn up some great results. It's a fascinating topic, and I did my best to portray it accurately.

Monsters: An Investigator's Guide to Magical Beings by John Michael Greer. This is my unofficial textbook on the supernatural in this series. Greer's book inspired the concept of a spiritual werewolf, and many other concepts. A must-read for those interested in the paranormal.

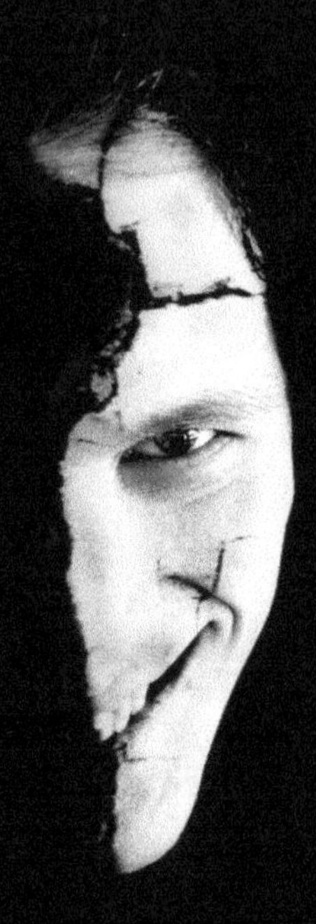

AYZZ   JBME   NUSL
KDGH   EWQG   FVXY
YBDFF

About the Author

~

Edison T. Crux is a storyteller, devoted husband, loving daddy, and coffee enthusiast. He grew up in Beloit, WI, living in a haunted house across the street from a cemetery. Although his writing can be dark or serious, in person Edison is a very upbeat and silly guy. He currently lives with his wife and children in Beloit, WI.

Contact the Author
edison@wisconsinwerewolf.com

Find Edison on
Facebook, Google+, Twitter, & YouTube.